D0122439

Sources for Library Materials in FY10
Albany County Public Library

- Cash Gifts
- Public Money
- Donated Items

18%
50%
32%

"I just came up with a fantastic idea. When school starts in the fall, I think you should run for class president!" Laurel exclaimed. "With the promise that you'll try your best to put an end to dork discrimination!"

"Wow. You're right—that *is* a fantastic idea!" I replied. "For someone *else* to do. Not me."

She gave me one of her super-serious, sincere looks—like the kind she used in the Don't Let People Starve PSAs. "You have the opportunity to be the savior of not just all the kids at the Center for Creative Learning, but of anyone who has ever been teased. Or tripped. Or friend-dumped."

After everything I had been through over the last few years—my parents' divorce, being friend-dumped, moving, getting a brand-new family, becoming a little sister, being about to become a big sister—only now was I starting to feel like things were leveling out. (Well, as level as they could get when you lived with the most famous girl in the world.)

Let someone else's life be turned upside down for a while.

I needed a break.

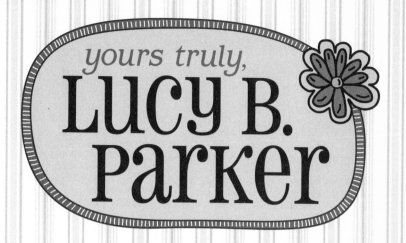

yours truly, LUCY B. PARKER

vote for me!

ROBIN PALMER

G. P. Putnam's Sons
An Imprint of Penguin Group (USA) Inc.

G. P. PUTNAM'S SONS
A division of Penguin Young Readers Group.
Published by The Penguin Group.
Penguin Group (USA) Inc., 375 Hudson Street, New York, NY 10014, U.S.A.
Penguin Group (Canada), 90 Eglinton Avenue East, Suite 700,
Toronto, Ontario M4P 2Y3, Canada (a division of Pearson Penguin Canada Inc.).
Penguin Books Ltd, 80 Strand, London WC2R 0RL, England.
Penguin Ireland, 25 St. Stephen's Green, Dublin 2, Ireland
(a division of Penguin Books Ltd.).
Penguin Group (Australia), 250 Camberwell Road, Camberwell,
Victoria 3124, Australia (a division of Pearson Australia Group Pty Ltd).
Penguin Books India Pvt Ltd, 11 Community Centre, Panchsheel Park,
New Delhi - 110 017, India.
Penguin Group (NZ), 67 Apollo Drive, Rosedale, Auckland 0632,
New Zealand (a division of Pearson New Zealand Ltd).
Penguin Books (South Africa) (Pty) Ltd, 24 Sturdee Avenue,
Rosebank, Johannesburg 2196, South Africa.
Penguin Books Ltd, Registered Offices: 80 Strand, London
WC2R 0RL, England.

Published simultaneously in Canada.
Printed in the United States of America.

Design by Kristin Smith.
Text set in Lomba.
Library of Congress Cataloging-in-Publication Data is available upon request.

ISBN 978-0-399-25629-5
1 3 5 7 9 10 8 6 4 2

For my brother Josh,
who did not look like a raisin when he was born

Acknowledgments

As always, immense gratitude to everyone at Penguin, most of all, Jennifer Bonnell, *ne plus ultra* of editors. And a special thanks to Lisa Silfen and Chris Linn at MTV, who, after I've been holed up writing all morning, make me laugh all afternoon.

yours truly,
LUCY B. Parker
vote for me!

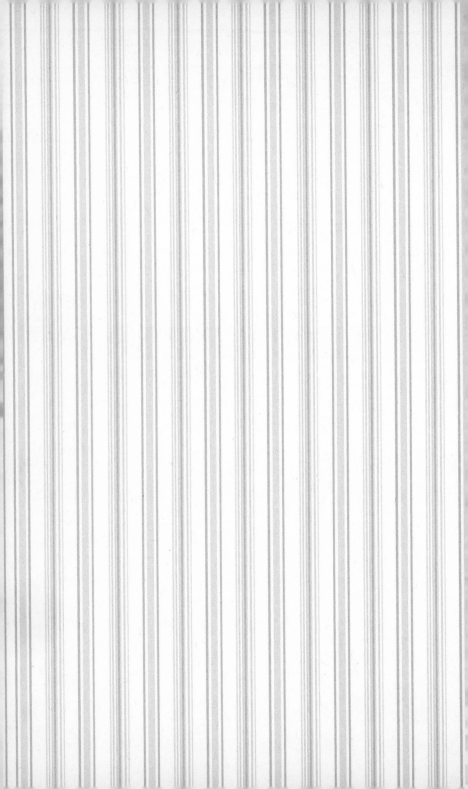

chapter 1

Dear Dr. Maude,

I know you haven't heard from me for a while. (42 days since my last e-mail to you, in case you're counting.) Unlike some people—i.e., the person whose bedroom is next to mine, aka Laurel Moses, Superstar—I am not in L.A. shooting a movie. And unlike my two (okay, only) friends Beatrice and Alice, I'm not away at camp. I'm here in New York City. In the same apartment building as you. With no one to talk to except Pete, our doorman.

Besides my trip to L.A. to hang out with Laurel while she worked on her movie, it's been a pretty boring summer. Yes, I've gotten to spend a lot of non–dentist appointment/ bra-shopping QT (quality time) with Mom. Which, if you remember from one of my previous e-mails, had been a problem because I had been feeling ignored by her ever since we moved here from Northampton, Massachusetts.

But, to be honest, I'm a little sick of her, especially because, ever since Alan bought her this book called How to Become a Well-Rounded, Cultured New Yorker in Thirty Days, she's decided that our QT should be spent going to all the different museums listed in the book. This is my summer vacation—I'm not supposed to have to LEARN things every day. I'm supposed to be doing FUN things like swimming and riding bikes, two things that are lot easier to do in Northampton than here in Manhattan.

The good news is that in a few days I'll be able to go ride bikes and swim all I want because I'm going up to spend some QT with my dad. It's probably going to be one of our last QTs before my brother The Creature is born in November. Technically I should be calling him Ziggy, because that's the crazy name Dad and Sarah, his girlfriend, are planning on giving the baby. But I'm practicing some positive thinking (because she's a yoga teacher, Sarah's way into that) by NOT calling him that and just sticking with The Creature until they get it together and come up with a normal name. Otherwise, he'll be teased forever and his life will be a total mess and he'll have to go on your TV show *Come on, People—Get with the Program* for advice about how to fix it.

I'm really excited to hang out with my dad. Ever since Mom and I moved here in April so we could be with Alan and Laurel (BTW—can you believe the most famous girl in the world is going to be my stepsister? I still can't) I've seen him only once. Even after the divorce, I still got to see him whenever I wanted because he moved only a few blocks away. And as much as I like New York, I guess I'm just missing home. Even though, when I came back to New York from L.A., New York felt like home, too.

But getting back to why you haven't heard from me in so long. Now that I live with Laurel, I know how busy a person can get when she's famous. I mean, you're not as famous as she is (did you hear that *In Touch with People* magazine named her Most Famous Teen Superstar of All Time last week?), but between your show, and the fact that you're a *New York Times*–bestselling author, and that infomercial you do for wrinkle cream, you're still pretty famous.

But still, just because a person is famous doesn't mean that she doesn't have to practice common courtesy—like, say, taking the time to send at least ONE e-mail back to a fan. Especially if that fan has written the famous person 31 VERY LONG e-mails (32, including this one).

I know you're probably saying, "Look, you're only twelve years old, and while you might THINK you have problems, you really don't, which is why I have to spend my time focusing on the adults who do." But not being able to get your boobs to stop growing or the fact that you can't figure out who to have as a local crush on ARE big problems.

Remember I told you about how Beatrice says there's a three-crush rule? How you have to have a local one, a long-distance/vacation one, and a celebrity one? Well, I still don't have any. Yes, I may have kissed Connor Forrester in L.A., but he's definitely NOT my long-distance and/or celebrity one. We're friends, but frankly I find him too goofy to have a crush on.

That being said, seeing that I am the keeper of the recently started Official Crush Log of the Girls at the Center for Creative Learning in N.Y.C. (to go along with the Official Period Log of the Girls at the Center for Creative Learning in N.Y.C.—I decided to make it school-wide instead of just focusing on my grade), it doesn't look good that I don't have any crushes to put in there. OR that I still don't have my period. I'm still kind-of, sort-of considering Beatrice's brother Blair for the local crush position, but I'm going to have to wait until I see him after he comes home from camp to see if I feel any crush symptoms before being sure.

Personally, I think this crush stuff is overrated. I mean, what's so great about having one crush, let alone three? I'm sure right now you're probably saying, "Well, Lucy, if you feel that way, then why did you start a log?" And the answer to that would be that while I may be a little (okay, a lot) on the unorganized side when it comes to my bedroom, I feel very strongly that there are certain things that need to be kept organized in case anyone needs certain information. Like, say, about crushes. Or periods. Even if Cristina Pollock, the meanest/most popular girl in my grade thinks it's stupid and calls me Period Girl because of it.

But getting back to the crush thing. Maybe if I had it easy, like Laurel, I'd be a little more into it. See, she gets to have Austin Mackenzie as all three of her crushes. Local (when they're in the same city like for movies or awards shows), long distance (when he's in L.A. and she's in N.Y.C.), and celebrity (as you probably know, he's the boy equivalent of her). And not only is he her crush, but he's also her boyfriend, because they totally fell for each other when we were in L.A.

Anyway, I hope you and your dachshunds Id and Ego are doing okay. I still keep hoping I'll run into the three of you in the lobby. Even though doormen are supposed to protect the privacy of the people who live in the building, Pete told me that you're in town instead of away on summer vacation. (Don't worry—the only reason he told me is because we're really, really good friends, and he knows how much I want to meet you.)

Oh, I keep meaning to ask you—do you have any hobbies? I don't. But I think I'm going to make that one of my resolutions for the school year—to get some hobbies. That, and to get my period.

Hope to hear from you soon.

yours truly,
LUCY B. PARKER

A few days later, as I was packing for my trip to Dad's (really just shoving all my clothes into a duffel bag as quickly as possible before Mom could come in and say, "Lucy, how many times do I have to tell you that that's NOT the way we pack around here! We FOLD the clothes NEATLY so that they don't get all WRINKLED!"), I came up with another resolution: "No matter how mean a person has been to you, try being nice to them and see if that makes them be a little nicer."

That one I wasn't going to wait until school began to start working on. I was planning on putting it into use during the trip in case I ran into my ex-BFFs Rachel and

Missy, the ones who dumped me three days before sixth grade started. Over the PHONE from the mall.

If I did run into them, instead of ignoring them and pretending they didn't exist, I would have what Mom calls a BPM (Bigger Person Moment). I'd just walk straight up to them and say, "Hi, guys. How are you?"

It's not like I would try and become BFFs again with them, because (a) I already had two new BFFs: Laurel and Beatrice, and (b) Missy and Rachel had been so awful to me that they barely deserved me TALKING to them letting alone the re-friending thing. But at least it would clear the air and hopefully give me some good karma, which is something that my parents are big on. They're both Buddhists and say that karma is kind of like luck. And if you do good things in this lifetime, then your karma is good for the next one, when you're reincarnated. Basically, it's like extra credit points on a test.

A little while later, after changing three times before finally settling on my new Minnie Mouse T-shirt, a denim miniskirt, red knee socks, and black Chuck Taylors (the red and black matched the T-shirt), I walked from my apartment on Central Park West and Seventy-sixth Street down to Seventy-second to catch the crosstown M72 bus. Laurel and I were going to have a Welcome-Home-to-Her/Bon-Voyage-to-Me lunch at Synchronicity 4, our favorite restaurant. Once I was settled in my seat, I reached into my I ♥ NY tote bag for my Bonne Bell Coconut Cake Lip Smacker and smothered it on my lips.

According to Mom, Lip Smackers had been around since she was my age, but I had only recently discovered them at Claire's. The minute I tried the Cookie Dough one, I was totally addicted. Of the bazillion flavors, I already had twelve, which was two more than the number of pairs of Converses I owned. Not only do they do a great job keeping your lips soft, but if you're the kind of person who gets hungry a lot, they're doubly awesome because of their dessert, soda, Starburst, and Skittles collections.

After I made sure the cap was on tightly (lint-covered Lip Smackers = disgusting), I took out my "Important Pieces of Advice" notebook. It used to be called "Important Pieces of Advice People Have Given Me," but I changed it on account of the fact that I was coming up with a lot of the advice myself. Like, say, "Bigger Person Moments (BPMs) lead to better karma," which is what I wrote down right then. And "Make sure you double-check to make sure the cap on your Lip Smacker is on tight before you put it in your bag."

After the old woman sitting next to me told me that she liked my outfit, I wrote, "Don't be afraid to wear lots of color." Color is very important to me. Unfortunately, some people (i.e., Cristina Pollock) don't appreciate it. In fact, I had once heard her tell her BFF Marni that I looked like a crayon box had thrown up on me.

As usual, Synchronicity was packed. Not only were they world famous for their frozen peanut butter hot chocolate, but after Laurel recently made the mistake of telling a reporter it was her favorite restaurant in New York, it got even more crowded.

I'm here, I texted Laurel. *Where r u?*

Next to the statue of the moon, she texted back.

I looked over to see a girl with frizzy red hair, buck teeth, and thick-lensed black-rimmed glasses wearing a lavender shirt and overalls. I sighed. If they had given out awards for Most Dramatic Change from One of the World's Most Beautiful Teens to Total and Complete Dork, Laurel totally would've won it, because there was no way anyone would've recognized her at that moment.

Back when she had been in Northampton shooting a movie when our parents first started dating, I had taken her to the Holyoke Mall so she could experience what it was like to be a normal kid. At the time, I had suggested that we make her look nerdy so there wouldn't be a giant stampede if they recognized her. Ever since then, she's gotten *really* into wearing disguises when we go on our IBSs (Individual Bonding Sessions—this thing Alan had come up with so that we could blend our family together faster). At first it had mostly been hats (luckily, I had a very large collection of them), but then she started adding glasses, and wigs, and really ugly clothes from the thrift stores that I dragged her to. In the beginning she hated thrift stores because she had an issue with germs, but soon she came to love them. Well, after Annie, the woman who owned our dry cleaner, assured her that the chemicals they used would get rid of any grossness without harming the environment. But the fake buck teeth were new. Not to mention a little scary.

I made my way over. "Hey, Laurel."

She looked around nervously. "I don't know who you're talking to. My name is Jane." Jane Austen was Laurel's pseudonym, which is a fake name you use when you're trying to disguise your identity, like at hotels and stuff. In Laurel's case, it was also the name of her favorite writer, some British lady who lived over two hundred years ago. Apparently, she was pretty famous, so it seemed like a weird name to choose if you were trying to stay anonymous.

"Okay. Hi, *Jane*. What happened to your teeth? They're so . . . *buck*."

"Aren't they great?" she whispered excitedly as she took them out and shoved them toward me. "I had the prop guy on the movie make them when I was in L.A." One of the good things about being a star was that if you were nice—like Laurel was—then you could get all sorts of free stuff from the prop and wardrobe department. I couldn't *wait* for Halloween.

I leaned back and cringed. "Laurel, I know we're fristers and all, but I don't need to touch your teeth," I whispered, pushing them back toward her. Out of the corner of my eye I could see a Japanese man wearing an I ♥ NY T-shirt with a camera strap around his neck looking very confused. "Put those back in," I ordered. "You're scaring the tourists."

To be honest, she was starting to scare *me*. Before I knew it, she was going to do something really gross, like add a fake mole to her face. Which, I knew from my old teacher Mrs. Kline, was very hard to look at. Especially if there were hairs growing out of it.

I looked around the packed restaurant. "How long is the wait?"

"I'm not sure," she replied. "The hostess told me forty-five minutes, but when the girl who got here right after me asked, I heard her say twenty."

I sighed. "Uh-oh."

"What?"

"I hate to tell you this," I said, "but you've been the victim of . . . *dork discrimination*." DD, as Beatrice and I called it, was when you were ignored in stores or picked last in gym because of things like having bad skin, or wearing Christmas sweaters in February.

Her eyes widened. "I have?" Laurel may have been really smart when it came to choosing movie roles, but when it came to real-life regular kid stuff? Not so much.

I nodded. "I'm afraid so."

Her face fell. "Wow. It feels really . . . *awful*."

"Yeah, I know," I agreed. Even though I didn't own any Christmas-related clothing, I, too, had been DD'd against at times. Especially by Cristina Pollock.

Some of it probably had to do with the fact that I had turned down her invitation to sit with her at lunch after she found out I lived with Laurel. But it was more than that. Cristina was Popular-with-a-capital-P, and I was Not-popular-with-a-capital-N. While she had 742 friends on Facebook, I had only 275. And thirty of them were kids I didn't even know from countries like Slovakia and Malaysia, who friended me only because we had Laurel in common.

"I had no idea dork discrimination was so widespread," Laurel said, concerned. "I mean, I know from what you've told me about Cristina that it goes on in school cafeterias and stuff, but I didn't realize it also happens in nice restaurants in Manhattan. Maybe I should talk to my agent about doing a public service announcement about it." Laurel did a lot of PSAs for things like the environment and animals that needed to be adopted, which I'm sure scored her major points with the karma thing.

"That's a good idea, but in the meantime, I'm going to do my part to try and end it right now." I grabbed her arm. "C'mon."

I marched us over to the hostess, who, like most New Yorkers, was dressed all in black. (Beatrice was like that, too, which drove me nuts.) "Excuse me," I said sweetly as Laurel hung back. "Could you tell me how long the wait for a table is?"

She looked down at the list on her clipboard before giving me a smile. But even when she did that, almost nothing on her face moved. According to Mom, that was because of something called Botox, which I once heard her tell Alan when I was overlistening was something that women who were scared of getting older put in their skin. "Only about fifteen minutes," she said.

Mom calls my overlistening eavesdropping, but personally, I find that to be a very ugly word. It's not my fault that I have extra-fantastic hearing and seem somehow always to end up standing in a spot that allows me to hear conversations I'm not supposed to.

"Really? That's great!" I said. I pulled Laurel up so she was next to me. "But if that's the case, how come you told my friend here that it would be a forty-five-minute wait?"

Her face went blank again. "Did I?" she asked nervously.

"Yeah, you did," I replied. "Which seems like a weird thing to say. I mean, that kind of sounds like . . . I don't know . . . *discrimination* or something."

A little bit of nervousness flickered across her face.

"Not that I have any idea why you'd discriminate against her," I said innocently. I leaned in. "I know she's not as pretty and cool-looking as someone like, say . . . Laurel Moses—"

"Oh, I just *love* Laurel Moses!" she exclaimed. Her song 'Millions of Miles' makes me cry every time."

"Yeah, anyway," I continued. "See, you can't *not* seat someone because you don't like the way she looks," I went on. "I'm not a lawyer, but the guy who's about to become my stepfather is, and I'm pretty sure if I asked him, he'd say that's ... *illegal.*"

The hostess got so upset, some lines actually appeared on her forehead. She grabbed two menus. "This has all been a misunderstanding," she said nervously. "See that empty table right over there?" she asked, pointing to a table smack in the middle of the restaurant.

See it? That was their VIP table, and I had actually *sat* at it, when I had come here with Laurel on a day when she was dressed as her regular superstar self. "I'm going to put you guys right there," she said with a smile. She lowered her voice. "Not only that, but your meal will be on the house."

I turned to Laurel. "What do you think, *Jane*?"

"I don't know," Laurel said. "I suddenly seem to have lost my appetite."

"Yeah, I know what you mean," I said. "I kind of feel like just getting a hot dog in the park or something." I grabbed Laurel's hand. "C'mon. Let's go."

When we got outside, Laurel turned to me. "Lucy— that was awesome! It totally reminded me of the episode I won the Emmy for—the Very Special one when Madison gave that speech in the cafeteria about how awful it was that people were acting like the quarterback she had a crush on totally no longer existed now that he had been in a car accident and couldn't play football anymore." Because Madison had a new crush every week, it was hard to keep them straight, but I did remember that one because it was a lot more serious than most of the episodes.

"Thanks," I said bashfully as we walked down Third Avenue. It wasn't like I wanted to be an actress or anything (although recently I had been thinking that maybe having my own advice-giving show like Dr. Maude could be cool), but still, that was a big compliment coming from her.

She stopped walking. "Wait a second—I just came up with a fantastic idea. When school starts in the fall, I think you should run for class president!" she exclaimed. "With the promise that you'll try your best to put an end to dork discrimination!"

"Wow. You're right—that *is* a fantastic idea!" I replied. "For someone *else* to do. Not me."

"Why not? Just a few minutes ago you were going on about how it's such a big problem!"

I took out my advice notebook. "'*Remember that everything you say can—and will—be used against you,*'" I said aloud as I wrote.

"I'm not using it against you—I'm just *reminding* you about how you convinced me that it was such a big problem!"

"Thanks, but the answer is still no."

"How come?"

"Hmm, let's see...." I said. "Well, there's the fact that according to Beatrice, Cristina Pollock has been class president ever since, like, kindergarten," I suggested. "And there's the fact that she hates me. And the fact that if I run against her, she'll hate me even more."

She gave me one of her super-serious, sincere looks—like the kind she used in the Don't Let People Starve PSAs. "But think of the millions of kids you could help—"

"But there're only a hundred fifty-seven kids in my grade," I said, confused.

She started to pace. "I know, but I'm talking big picture here, Lucy. You have the opportunity to be the savior of not just all the kids at the Center for Creative Learning, but of anyone who has ever been teased. Or tripped. Or friend-dumped." Her eyes narrowed. "Or made to wait for an hour in a very hot monkey costume so you get super-sweaty and look disgusting when the camera starts rolling because the guest star on that week's episode of your series thinks you were flirting with her boyfriend, which you totally were not."

She stopped in front of me. "Think about it—you have the opportunity to be a role model for an *entire generation* of lower-school girls."

I took out my advice notebook again. "*People who do a lot of public speaking because they're famous tend to be very good at convincing other people of things, so watch out*," I wrote. "I don't know," I said doubtfully. "That sounds cool, but it's also a lot of pressure. Especially since I heard next year is going to be *really hard* because of algebra—"

"Lucy, *you* are the chosen one. The one who can lead us out of the darkness."

My left eyebrow raised. "Isn't that what that old Native American guy said to Austin in that movie we watched on cable the other day—the one where he saves the world with the help of that Saint Bernard after the asteroid hits Earth?" While Connor's costars tended to be monkeys, Austin's were dogs a lot of the time.

She thought about it. "Huh. So that's why it sounds familiar." She shrugged. "But still, your country needs you, Lucy. The Cristina Pollocks of the world need to be stopped. Otherwise, they'll get married to the cutest guys in school, and there'll be a whole new generation of Mean Girls ruining people's reputations on Facebook and trashing them on gossip blogs just because they're mad they didn't get as many close-ups."

I cringed. I hadn't even thought about the new generation of Mean Girls that would result if people like Cristina Pollock had children. That would be awful.

"So if you can't do it for you, Lucy, do it for *us*—your fellow men and womenkind!" she said passionately. "Do it for the ones who aren't as brave as you. Who don't have the guts to stand up for what's right and put a stop to meanness."

Wow. If the acting thing ever stopped working, Laurel could totally get a job as a speechwriter for the president.

"Nice try," I said. "But the answer is still no."

With that, her eyes got all big and wet-looking, like tears were about to start falling from them any second. She *knew* I was a sucker for that. It was the same look she gave in the PSA for the ASPCA about animals that needed to be adopted.

"And don't you dare give me the ASPCA look." I glanced away as I shook my head again. "I agree it needs to be stopped—but not by me."

After everything I had been through over the last few years—my parents' divorce, being friend-dumped, moving, getting a brand-new family, becoming a little sister, being about to become a big sister—only now was I starting to feel like things were leveling out. (Well, as level as they could get when you lived with the most famous girl in the world.)

Let someone else's life be turned upside down for a while.

I needed a break.

chapter 2

Dear Dr. Maude,

You know how I told you I was really excited to go back to Northampton and hang out with my dad? Well, that was a mistake. Because so far the trip has been awful. In fact, I'm writing this to you on my iTouch from the bathroom of Frankie's Pizzeria after having spent the last five minutes in here crying.

If you've ever been to Frankie's (which I don't think you have, because Frankie always makes the famous people autograph a napkin that he then tacks up on the wall behind the cash register), you'd know that a person would have to be in REALLY bad shape to stay in the restroom at Frankie's for any longer than necessary because it smells disgusting.

I'm not sure what's going on, Dr. Maude. Ever since we moved I've been looking forward to coming back here. But from the second we got here this afternoon, I feel like everything's . . . different. And not good-different. BAD-different. Especially with my dad.

Okay, I just started crying again, which is not good. Do you think I might possibly be having a nervous breakdown? Because my friend Marissa (you remember her, right? She's the annoying one from Northampton) once told me that when her aunt had a nervous breakdown, she cried nonstop for days. Although if it is a nervous breakdown, that would definitely bring on my period, don't you think?

I'll Google "warning signs of a nervous breakdown" when I get back to Dad's house, but if you could get back to me about this before then, I'd appreciate it.

Thanks very much.

yours truly,
LUCY B. Parker

The weirdness started during the car ride up. Usually during long car rides with Mom, we had to listen to all this old music by people named Joni Mitchell and Carole King and Crosby, Stills, Nash, and Young. Not only that, but she'd sing along, and her voice is only the teensiest bit better than mine, and mine happens to be awful. So awful that Ms. Edut, my chorus teacher, asked me to mouth the words during our assemblies rather than sing them. Because of all the QT Mom and I had been spending together, I was actually looking forward to having the music on so we didn't have to talk. But she didn't put it on—not even when she finally calmed down after we got out of the city and onto I 95.

I'm not a big fan of silence. When it's really quiet, it's like the volume on the chatter in my brain gets turned up really loud, and I hear things, like "Your boobs are too big." Or "You really need to find someone to have a crush on before school starts again so that people don't think you're weird." Or "I know you and Laurel have been getting along well since the trip to L.A., but what if one day she wakes up and suddenly decides she'd rather hang out with someone with better coordination?"

Because I didn't want to listen to my brain's latest podcast about how the hair on my arms is too dark and makes me look like a monkey, I reached for the knob to turn the radio on.

"Honey, leave it off, okay?" Mom asked.

I turned to her. Mom hated silence almost as much as I did. She said it was because of her adult-onset ADHD. "How come?"

"So we can talk."

Uh-oh. Those four words were never good. Over the last year, whenever my parents said they had something to talk to me about, it usually ended up with me finding out my mother was dating Laurel Moses's father and we were moving to New York, or that, come fall, I'd have a new brother or sister. "You're not going to tell me you're pregnant, are you?" I demanded. Even though she was already forty-seven, if she had been getting shots in her butt like Mrs. Walker in 8F did, it could still happen. And Mrs. Walker had *triplets*!

"Lucy, I keep telling you this store is closed," she said, patting the area below her belly that I knew from health class was called the uterus. "Now please stop asking me that." Since we'd moved to New York, Mom had become a little less funky-Indian-shirts-and-ugly-Birkenstock-sandals and more Mom-looking. Not only that, but she had let Roger, Laurel's hairdresser, chop off her long brown curls into a longish bob. ("I'm sorry, but after forty-five, unless you're some crazy artist type, hair that long on a woman just *does not* work," he said with a sniff.) But even with her new momlike look, she still looked young enough to have a baby.

"So what do you want to talk to me about?" I asked warily.

"I just wanted to have a check-in," she replied. "To see how you're feeling about going back to Northampton."

I turned to her. "What do you mean, how do I feel? I feel great. I've been excited to go back and visit ever since we left."

"That's great, sweetie. I guess I just wanted to say I think it's important that you"—she paused—"*manage your expectations* about the weekend," she said.

"What does that mean?" Whenever Mom paused before saying something—especially something I wasn't familiar with, like this expectations thing—I knew I was about to get a lecture.

"Well, sometimes when we leave a place and we go

back to visit, we think that everything's going to be the same," Mom explained. "That nothing's changed—"

"It's only been four months. Nothing's changed," I said. "Other than Sarah getting really fat because she can't stop eating." I wondered if she'd have zits. I knew she was pregnant and all, but if she was going to eat so much junk food, she really should have to break out like the rest of us.

"Well, I just want you to be prepared, because while things may look the same, it will probably feel different. And that's not a bad thing. In fact, it's a good thing, because it means that the river of life is flowing and—"

I cringed. "Mom, please don't start with the river-of-life thing—" That was something she had gotten from one of the How-to-Blend-a-Family-in-Such-a-Way-That-People-Get-Along-Rather-Than-Spend-All-Their-Time-Alone-in-Different-Rooms-Watching-TV books she was always reading.

"Okay, fine," she said, "what I'm trying to say is that just as there are seasons to life—"

The seasons-of-life lecture was almost as bad as the river one. "I've only been gone a few months," I said, cutting her off as I punched the radio button. "And I get to hang out with Dad. How different can it be?"

Um, try *a lot*.

While I had loved Dad's loft over on Main Street, I was excited to finally see the house he and Sarah had bought on Maple Street. In the pictures Dad had e-mailed me, it looked great. I especially loved the photo of the guest room—aka my room. I couldn't wait to look out at the big elm tree in the yard when I woke up in the morning.

Which, I found out as soon as we arrived, was not going to be happening.

"You're making me sleep on a *sofa bed*?! In the *living room*?" I cried as we stood in front of a big tan couch with Indian-looking jewel-toned silk pillows.

"Honey, it's very comfortable," Dad said.

I turned to him. "How do you know?" I demanded. "Have you slept on it?"

"Well, no," he confessed. "But the guy at the store assured me it was."

I squinted. "Wait a minute—is your ponytail shorter?" Dad had had long hair ever since college. Some people thought it was weird, but in Northampton, it was pretty normal. Especially for a photographer like him.

He nodded. "Yeah. I had Deanna trim about two inches off." Deanna was Mom's BFF and the person whose house she was staying at. In a *real bed*.

What was going on here? Part of what made my parents my parents was that they were a little weird-looking. Now, since the divorce, and the move, and the baby coming, they were both becoming so ... *normal*. Sure, some of the stuff they did was completely embarrassing, but I *liked* that they didn't have parentlike hair and clothes. It made me feel a little more normal about not feeling normal.

I didn't say anything about the hair issue just then. There were more important things to deal with. Like my bed. "But why can't I sleep in the guest room?" I asked as Sarah came waddling in dressed in some long embroidered Indian-looking dress that, because she was so huge, made her look like she was wearing a tent. Now *she* was someone who could've used a bit more normalness. As she ripped open a package of Twinkies, I cringed. I loved junk food as much as the next person, but even *I* wouldn't go near a Twinkie. You might as well squirt dishwashing liquid in your mouth.

While Dad's hair was shorter, Sarah's long red braid was even longer. But her face had gotten so puffy, you couldn't even see the rhinestone stud on the side of her nose. It just sort of disappeared into the side. "Because it's Ziggy's room now," she said. "It turns out that the other bedroom we were thinking of putting him in isn't positioned well from a feng shui aspect." Feng shui is this Chinese thing about positioning furniture and stuff for good luck.

"Then I'll just sleep there," I said.

"Well, it's positioned well from a prosperity point of view, which is why it's now my studio," Dad said. "So you can't."

"But The Crea—I mean the *baby*—hasn't even been *born* yet and therefore doesn't actually *need* the room right now," I said.

"Lucy, we've been over this—his name is Ziggy," Dad

24

said firmly. "I keep telling you, it's very important for his emotional growth that you call him by his name instead of referring to him as 'the baby.' The books say it will help with his self-esteem."

What about *my* self-esteem? Having a brother named Ziggy was just plain embarrassing. And he wasn't even *born* yet.

As Sarah plopped down on the couch—aka my bed—I got a look at her legs. Which you kind of couldn't miss on account of the fact that they were so swollen they looked like tree trunks. She didn't even have ankles anymore. "If you had come last week, you absolutely could have stayed in there," she said, "but now that it's been saged, we really want to keep the space as undisturbed as possible so that when he arrives, Ziggy's aura and karma don't get contaminated."

Saging was when you walked around with a bundle of lit sage to clear a space of negative energy. Sarah liked to do it, a lot. I looked over at Dad. I didn't know what bothered me more—that he had fallen in love with someone so weird, or that he didn't say, "Listen, Sarah, you're more than welcome to be weird when my daughter isn't here, but we're not making her sleep on the couch." But he was busy reading the directions to the new baby swing and didn't even notice I was trying to get his attention.

"In fact," Sarah said, hoisting herself off the couch,

"we should probably smudge you, too." She ambled into the kitchen and returned a moment later with a smudge stick.

As she lit it and waved it around me, I began to sneeze. "I don't have negative energy!" I cried between sneezes. That was almost as bad as having B.O.

"Of course *you* don't," she agreed. "But walking around the streets of New York, you never know what you're picking up. And Ziggy's immune system isn't strong enough to ward off all that."

"Are you also going to tell me that I'm not going to be able to use the *bathroom* so that I don't screw up his karma when you give birth to him in the bathtub?" I asked. That was another thing that was big in the yoga world—making poor babies be born in the water. Which, if you asked me, was totally unfair. What if they didn't *like* the water because in a past life they had had a bad experience in the ocean when the waves were so strong that the top of their bathing suit fell down in front of a crowd of people or something?

Dad looked up from the swing. "Of course you can use the bathroom!" He looked over at Sarah. "Right?"

She smiled. "Of course! But if you could run the essential oil diffuser with some citrus oil in it afterward to purify the air, I'd appreciate it."

This was just great. My brother wasn't even born yet and already everything was revolving around him. It's not like I was expecting a parade with a huge banner that said WELCOME HOME, LUCY B. PARKER, but it would've been nice to feel welcome in own *father's* house.

The entire conversation at dinner was about Ziggy. What kind of preschool he should go to. At what age should they sign him up for swimming lessons. Should they have him circumcised at the hospital, or at some Jewish ceremony at home called a bris even though neither Dad nor Sarah was Jewish? At that, I got so grossed out I couldn't finish my third slice of Hawaiian pizza, even though it was my favorite kind. After that I drew the line and told them that I had suddenly gotten very tired and could we please go home so I could go to sleep, even though it was only eight o'clock.

"Lucy, it's great to have you here," Sarah said as she helped me make up the sofa bed in between bites of an ice cream sandwich. "We've missed bonding with you."

"Me, too," I said as I reached for the clicker. Too bad the only bonding that was going on was with an unborn baby, though. At least *Pet Rescue 911* would make it so that the night wasn't a total waste. But just as the animal rescue team walked into an abandoned building to rescue a litter of pit bulls, the TV clicked off.

I turned to Sarah, who was holding the clicker in one hand and covering her belly with the other. "What are you doing?" I cried. "This is the best part!"

"Did your dad not tell you?" she asked. "Since the pregnancy, we have a no-violence rule in effect in the house."

"But *Pet Rescue 911* isn't violent," I corrected. "That would be *America's Worst Pet Owners.* This one is about *stopping* violence. Against animals."

Sarah patted her belly. "I don't like the idea of Ziggy being exposed to so much anxiety." She hoisted herself up and waddled over to the iPod dock and speakers. A moment later, the room was flooded with a sloshing noise. "Plus, we have a no-TV-after-nine rule. Instead, we listen to this."

Since when were there *rules* at Dad's? Yet another normal thing. That was one of the great things about having a father who was a creative type—he didn't like rules. The sloshing continued. "What's that noise?" I asked suspiciously.

"It's the sound of a giant bathtub. So that Ziggy feels comfortable and prepared when I give birth to him in the water. Don't you find it so relaxing?"

I crossed my legs. Actually, it made me feel like I needed to pee. *Badly.* "And how long do you listen to it?" I asked.

"Oh, we keep it on all night," she replied. "It's very soothing. You'll be amazed at how deeply you sleep."

Not if I'd be waking up all night so that I didn't wet the sofa bed. I reached for my tote bag. Okay, so I wouldn't watch TV. No big deal. I'd just read instead. And slather some M&M's Lip Smacker on my mouth since there were no decent desserts in the house because Sarah had eaten them all.

Sarah came over and plopped down beside me, lifting up her pajama top. "And now it's time for your quality time with Ziggy."

I put my book down. "Huh?"

Grabbing my hand, she put it on her stomach. "Ziggy, Lucy is here," she whispered. "It's time for the two of you to bond."

Nothing happened, other than the sloshing water making my bladder feel more full by the second.

She looked at me. "Why don't you start the conversation, Lucy?"

"Go ahead, Lucy," said Dad, who was now standing over us with a camera. "Talk to him."

I would have done anything to be back in New York right then. Even if it meant doing math homework, which anyone who knew me knew was my least favorite thing in the world to do. "Uh . . . hi," I said loudly. "This is Lucy B. Parker. Your . . . sister."

Sarah covered her belly. "Let's use an inside voice, please," she whispered. "I'm afraid of—"

"The anxiety thing," I finished. "Got it." I looked down at the giant belly again. Just then there was some movement. "Did he just kick?"

Sarah nodded.

Huh. That was kind of cool. But making me talk to a belly? Not so cool.

"So . . . how are you doing?" I asked. Could he even (a) hear me or (b) understand English? What if babies spoke some entirely different language before they were born? It's not like they'd remember and be able to tell you about it. "I guess it's probably pretty warm in there, huh? Good thing you don't have to worry about clothes."

"Oh, this is beautiful. Just beautiful!" Dad exclaimed as he wiped away a tear while snapping away.

Okay, that was it. I was *not* going to sit here with my hand on his girlfriend's belly, watching Dad cry. I gave the longest, fakest yawn I could muster. "I'm *reeeally* tired," I announced. "Must be the long drive. And the bonding. I think I need to go to sleep now."

"Of course," Dad said, giving me a hug.

I waited for Sarah to get up, but she just sat there. "Well . . . good night," I said.

"Aren't you forgetting someone?" she asked. She pointed to her belly. "A kiss for Ziggy?"

I looked at Dad. "It's one of our nightly rituals," he explained.

Knowing they wouldn't leave me alone until I did it, I leaned down and quickly planted a kiss on her stomach. But not so quickly that Dad didn't get a picture of it. "We're *so* framing that," Sarah said.

And I was *so* over this baby business.

"OMIGOD?! LUCY, IS IT YOU? IS IT REALLY, REALLY YOU?!" Marissa yelled as she ran into the Cupcake

Café the next day. (My favorite bakery in town, Sweet Lady Jane, had closed soon after I left. Probably because without me there, they lost a lot of business.) As Marissa smothered me in a hug, trailing behind her was a very tall, very skinny girl with long dark hair and the black Chuck Taylors with the white stars that I had been begging Mom for.

"Hey, Marissa," I said once I untangled myself from her. So at least some things never changed. Like Marissa's being totally annoying. And her hair being so red it was orange. And the way her breath smelled like chicken noodle soup.

Her eyes got huge. "OMIGOD, I CAN'T BELIEVE HOW BIG YOUR BOOBS GOT!" she shrieked.

"Marissa!" I cried as I turned as red as my Adopt-a-Sloth T-shirt. It wasn't like there were any boys around, but still.

She stuck her chest out. "See how much mine have grown?"

I squinted. They were still the size of mosquito bites.

"And that picture your dad put on your Facebook page of you kissing Sarah's belly? Omigod, that is SOOOOOO cute!"

I still couldn't believe he had done that without even bothering to ask me. Talk about embarrassing.

She turned to the tall girl. "Cass, this is Lucy—the girl I told you about. The Keeper of the Periods."

I turned even redder. Yes, it was true—she was referring to the period log I kept—but it's not like that needed to be the first thing a person found out about me.

31

"You can put me in as February 6," the girl said. "Eight twelve a.m."

"You know, I totally think I'm going to get mine this week," Marissa announced. She grabbed her stomach and doubled over. "I have horrible cramps," she moaned. When she stood up, she turned toward the girl. "Lucy still hasn't gotten hers, either."

I was so red I was probably purple. "Yeah, you told me," the girl said. Of *course* she had. Because that was a completely Marissa thing to do. "So are you going to put me in the log?" she asked. "Oh, and I was thinking—you should do a kissing log, too. Like when everyone's first kiss is and with who. Marissa told me about the crush log you're keeping, and that's okay and all, but I think the kissing one is a lot more interesting."

Who *was* this girl? And who had asked her for her opinion on what kind of logs I should keep anyway? "Um, don't take this the wrong way," I said, "but who *are* you?"

Marissa threw her arm around the girl's shoulder. "This is Cassandra Paraskevis. She just moved here. We met at the pool last week. And because our last names both start with P-A-R, she'll be sitting in front of me whenever we have to sit alphabetically."

"But I was the P-A-R in front of you," I said, a little hurt. Why was I upset? Back when Marissa used to sit behind me, she drove me nuts with the way she'd tap me on the shoulder every five seconds.

"Yeah, but you don't live here anymore," she replied. "So Cass is the new P-A-R, right, Cass?" Marissa turned to me. "Because we're BFFs, I get to call her Cass."

"You guys just met last week, and now you're BFFs?"

They nodded. If it were just Marissa nodding proudly, I'd think that maybe it was just her being her usual Marissa-self. But this Cassandra girl—Cass, to her BFFs, of which I was not one—looked equally psyched about the whole thing.

"You can't become BFFs with someone in a *week*," I said.

"Sure you can," Cassandra said. "It's like that whole love-at-first-sight thing that happens in movies."

"Ohhhh, I just *love* when that happens!" Marissa sighed.

"Me, too!" Cassandra squealed. "How did we not know we had that in common?!"

"It's like in that movie Laurel did—*The Walk Toward Tomorrow*—when she saw the boy across the bleachers in the gym and totally fell for him—"

"Only to discover he was dating the head cheerleader!" Cassandra squealed. "That's my all-time *favorite*."

"Mine, too," Marissa sighed.

I had to say, they were perfect for each other.

"Speaking of Laurel Moses," Cassandra said, "is it really weird living with her?"

I shrugged. "Not so much."

"Really? I mean, because she's so pretty and famous

and probably has a billion friends, and you're just—you know—so ... *regular.*"

Way to make a person feel bad. Especially a person who *did*, in fact, spend a lot of time worrying that her super-famous frister was going to dump her for being so regular-girl-like.

Marissa grabbed my iTouch. "I can't believe Alan got you one of those," she said. "After Ziggy's born and I'm babysitting him, I'm going to save up my money so I can get one, too." She threw her arm around Cassandra's shoulder. "That way I can e-mail Cass from wherever I am, which is very important for BFFs to be able to do." She patted my arm. "But don't worry—I'll e-mail you, too, sometimes."

"How are you going to babysit Ziggy?" I asked. "You barely know how to change a diaper." Marissa had told me that the only time she had changed a diaper was on her baby cousin Marshall, and she had pulled it so tight she had cut off his circulation and he had started screaming.

"I've been practicing on my old Baby Alive," she said. "By the way, did you know that the reason you have to burp babies is because if you don't, they can get a giant gas bubble in their stomach which can make it *explode*?"

My own stomach started getting all jumpy. I hadn't even ever *held* a real baby before, let alone changed a diaper. And if anyone had gotten a look at my old dolls before we gave them to Goodwill and saw how most of them were missing an arm or a leg or a head, they'd never let me hold one.

"And there's this spot on their head called the 'soft spot' where their skull hasn't gotten completely hard yet," she went on, "and it's right over their *brain,* so you have to make sure you don't push too hard on it or else it'll open up and everything in it will just *spill right out.*"

Grossed out, I pushed my red velvet cupcake away. In less than twenty-four hours, I had had two meals ruined. It's not like the cupcake was that good anyway (definitely not as good as Billy's Bakery in New York City) but still, it wasn't fair.

How come no one had told me this stuff before? Because of my coordination problems, I had already been worried about dropping Ziggy, but after what Marissa just said . . . What if I was so nervous my hands got all sweaty like Alan's and they slipped and I pushed on that soft spot and he got brain damage because of me? Sarah and Dad were pretty mellow because of all the yoga and Buddhism, but I'm pretty sure they'd freak out if I broke their baby. Hopefully, I could find some YouTube videos about how to hold a baby. Otherwise, I was in big trouble.

As if the trip couldn't get any worse, the minute we got to the town pool, who do I see sitting on the edge of the pool with sunglasses on dangling their feet in the water and trying to seem all Don't-we-look-like-we-should-be-on-a-TV-show? but Rachel and Missy.

"Oh great," I muttered under my breath as my heart started to speed up.

"Lucy—LOOK!" gasped Marissa. "IT'S RACHEL AND MISSY!"

As my obviously bad luck would have it, she was so loud that everyone turned around to look at us. Including, of course, Rachel and Missy.

Marissa turned to Cassandra. "Remember I told you about how Rachel and Missy and Lucy used to be BFFs? But then three days before sixth grade they called her from the mall and dumped her over the phone?"

Cassandra nodded. Of *course* Marissa had told her.

"Well, that's them right over there," Marissa announced, pointing at them. "Hi, Rachel! Hi, Missy!" she yelled, waving so hard it looked like her arm was going to fall off.

What was going on here? Sure, Marissa was annoying, but I had never known her to be *mean*. Which, the way she was about to put me face-to-face with the two people who had hurt me the most in my life, was what she was doing. But then, to my total surprise, not only did they wave back, they got up and started walking toward us. In bikinis. When did they start wearing bikinis? Last summer when we hung out here together, the three of us wore one-pieces. Which, underneath my clothes, was what I was still wearing. The only time I had had a bikini on my body was when Laurel and I went to a barbecue at Austin and Connor's house in L.A. and I had forgotten my swimsuit. And then I refused to take off my jeans and shirt, even though it was super-hot out.

Okay, just keep calm, I said to myself as I stood there. *And remember your be-nice-to-mean-people resolution. Even if you have no idea how you're going to be able to get a sentence out without bursting into tears.*

"Hey, Lucy," Rachel said, giving me a big braces-less smile. Yet another thing that had changed since I left. Actually, if you counted the way her boobs had finally grown, that was three things that had changed.

"How are you!?" Missy asked, giving me a hug. A hug? From the girl who dumped me over the phone from a mall?

"I'm fine?" I said, warily. I didn't trust her niceness for a second. Hold on—was she wearing eye shadow and mascara? At a pool? That just seemed like a waste of money. And when did they start looking like they belonged on an MTV show? And why were they being *nice* to me?

Missy stood back and looked at me. "Look at your T-shirt. It's so cute!"

I glanced down at my Adopt-a-Sloth T-shirt. "Thanks," I said. But now I *knew* something was up. She hated mammals like sloths and otters. She thought they looked slimy.

"How long are you in town for?" Rachel asked.

"Till Monday," I replied. This wasn't fair. I hadn't even gotten a chance to put my be-nice-to-mean-people resolution to the test because they weren't being mean to me.

"You should come hang out with us on Main Street later," she said.

"Why?" I blurted. Oh no. It was starting. When I was nervous, I blurted. I was pretty sure it was a medical condition. I waited to see if I was so nervous that I began bloversharing (that was a combination of blurting and oversharing, and it was *not* pretty). Luckily, I stayed silent.

"So we can hear all about New York!" Missy said.

I searched their faces to see if they were joking, but they looked normal. In fact, they looked just like they looked back when we were all friends. Except for the makeup and the boobs and the bikinis. I wracked my brain thinking of a good response ("Okay" seemed pretty boring, while "Are you kidding? After the way you treated me, I'd rather eat salmon, and you guys know how much I hate all seafood other than fried clams from Friendly's!" felt a little on the angry side). I heard Dad's voice in my head. *Lucy,* it said, *when you have the opportunity to forgive people, take it. Not only will it make you feel better, but it helps with your karma.*

"Okay," I said, feeling my stomach start to unclench a bit. "That sounds like fun," For this, I deserved some seriously awesome karma.

When Rose, our housekeeper, started going on and on about miracles, and how they could happen in an instant (this usually came up as we were watching some guy return from the dead on one of the Spanish *telenovela* soap operas we liked to watch together in the kitchen), I tended to zone out. Sure, I had experienced a few miracles in my life—like when I got an 88 on a mixed-fractions quiz after completely making up the answers because I hadn't studied—but the whole miracle thing seemed a little hokey to me. But that afternoon, as Rachel, Missy, and I browsed in Faces—one of my favorite stores on Main Street before those guys won it in the friend breakup— I started to think maybe there was something to this miracle business. Not only did all my nervousness go away, but I was relaxed to the point where I started putting on funny hats and glasses in a version of TWUO, aka The World's Ugliest Outfit, a game the three of us had made up in fourth grade. Maybe people *could* change. Or, in this case, change back to who they used to be. Maybe now that almost a year had gone by since they had dumped me, Rachel and Missy had gotten a lot more mature and had come to realize (a) what a great BFF I had been and (b) what total jerks they had been.

Afterward, as we sat at a table at Scoops, Rachel turned to me. "I totally forgot how good you are at coming up with ugly outfits!" She giggled. Yet another miracle—she rarely *ever* gave out compliments like that. As I thought about it, I realized that, actually, another miracle in my life had happened at Scoops—because it was there that I had run into Laurel one night and learned that even though she was a superstar, she still had to go through normal-people-like things, such as being dumped by *her* BFF.

"Thanks," I said proudly, trying not to eat my scoop of mint chocolate chip in one bite. I was feeling so good, it felt like a sundae kind of afternoon, but when Rachel and Missy ordered one scoop of frozen yogurt each (when did they start eating *that*?) I decided to stick to one scoop. Without even *one* topping, which took a huge amount of willpower.

"And those Lip Smackers are so cool," Missy said. "I'm so glad you pointed those out to us." Yet another miracle—I had been the one to discover something cool first. Not only that, but Faces ended up having the Cotton Candy Lip Smacker, which was very hard to find because it was so yummy.

The two of them looked at each other. "So . . . we heard you went to L.A.," Missy said.

"Actually, we read about it," Rachel corrected her. "On the gossip blogs." She leaned in. "We can't believe you got to kiss Connor Forrester!" she squealed. "You *have* to tell us what that was like!"

My stomach fell to my knees. *That's* what this was about. Boy, did I feel dumb. Here I was thinking that the two of them wanted to be friends with me again, but really all they wanted to know about was The Connor Thing. I knew that I was going to have to deal with that a lot when school started, but because I had spent most of the time since I had been back from L.A. doing QT things with Mom, I had been spared so far.

"Don't take this the wrong way or anything," Missy said, "but you and Connor Forrester seem like a *very* weird combination."

"Yeah," agreed Rachel. "It's like . . . peanut butter and . . . hot sauce."

She wasn't wrong. Anyone who knew me knew that the fact that my first kiss was with a super-cute, super-famous actor who used the word *dude* a lot was almost as unbelievable as the idea of Marissa suddenly acting normal and unannoying. I couldn't even say he was my type because I didn't even *have* a type. And because Connor was so famous—not quite Laurel Moses–famous or Austin Mackenzie–famous, but still up there—it had been all over the gossip blogs.

"He must be the coolest boyfriend ever," said Missy dreamily.

"He's *not* my boyfriend," I corrected her.

She leaned in. "Uh-huh. So has he been to visit you in New York? Have all your friends met him?"

"No-o," I replied. "Because like I said—*he's not my boyfriend*. We're just friends. Sometimes we have Triple S's, but that's all."

"What's a Triple S?" Rachel asked.

"A Skype Snack Session. We eat snacks together while Skyping. It's a friend thing, NOT a boyfriend thing! I don't even want a boyfriend!" I rambled. Uh-oh. Bloversharing. And to make it worse, part of the reason they had given for dumping me last year was that I didn't have a crush on anyone. Now they knew I didn't want a boyfriend!

"Do you have a seventh-grade dance at your school?" Rachel asked. "Are you going to ask him to be your date?"

"I *just* said I don't like him that way. Plus, he lives all the way in California."

"That would be *so* romantic!" Missy cried. She gasped. "Do you think he'll go to the junior prom with you?"

"Prom?!" I yelped. "That isn't for another five years!" What part of I-don't-like-him-like-that was in a different language?

"So Lucy, we were thinking . . ." Rachel said, "we know that we haven't been so good about staying in touch since you moved—"

Since I *moved*? How about staying in touch since they *dumped* me?

"—but the truth is we really, really miss you," Missy said. When she said that, I noticed that she blinked a lot. I knew from when we had been BFFs that was something she did when she was lying.

"Totally," Rachel agreed. "And because of that, we

were thinking that maybe we could come visit you in New York some time!"

"Yeah. Like maybe even when Connor happens to be there," Missy added.

"And maybe Laurel and Austin, too."

I looked at them.

As dumb as it sounded, and as mean as they had been to me, ever since the day they had dumped me, I had been waiting for them to apologize and say they missed me and wanted to be friends again. But now all I wanted was to get out of there. "Hmm, so you guys want to come to New York . . ."

They nodded. "We were thinking maybe Columbus Day weekend, because we have that Monday off," Rachel said. "Do you happen to know if Connor will be there?"

I shrugged. "I don't know. He might."

"Really?!" they squealed.

"But if he was," I continued, "I'm not sure he'd be all that into hanging out with you guys."

Their smiles fell at the same exact time. Maybe it was the completely-joined-at-the-hip, never-apart thing.

"See, once when we were Triple S'ing," I said, "Connor told me that the number one thing he hates more than anything—even more than undercooked French fries—are Mean People." Okay, so maybe we hadn't actually ever had that particular conversation, but I felt like I knew him well enough to know that if I had called him right then and said, "Hey, Connor—by any chance do you hate

Mean People?" he would've said, "Oh yeah. Totally, dude. Who doesn't?"

I stood up. "And the fact that you guys could treat me the way that you did, and then a year later *pretend* to be all nice and say that you missed me, when really you just want to hang out with famous people?" I shook my head. "That's pretty much the official definition of a Mean Person."

Wait a minute . . . This never happened. I, Lucy B. Parker, had just totally stood up for myself *in the moment, in front of the actual people who needed to be stood up to,* and not three weeks after the fact, alone, in front of my bedroom mirror!

I gathered up my stuff. "So while it was nice seeing you, I'm gonna go now."

"Wait a second," Rachel sputtered. "Are you turning down our offer to be friends again?"

"And did you just call us Mean People . . . *to our faces*?" Missy added.

"Let me think about that for a second," I said. "Yup. I'm pretty sure I did."

At the same moment, their mouths turned into little O's, which, now that Rachel's braces were gone, were also identical.

I flashed them a smile. "See you around," I said as I started walking away. I stopped and turned around. "Oh, and by the way? The Pink Lemonade and Wild Raspberry Lip Smackers you guys bought? I happen to know from experience that there are way better flavors than those."

I began walking again, and thankfully managed to make it to the door without my coordination issue flaring up. But once outside, I felt like I was going to faint. When you're not used to standing up for yourself, it can make you very light-headed and dizzy. I tried to get my breathing back to normal and reached into my tote bag for my advice notebook.

"*When you have the chance to stand up to a Mean Person, do it. If only to see the dumb expression on their face when you do,*" I wrote. "*And then RUN—as fast as possible.*"

Which is exactly what I did.

chapter 3

Dear Dr. Maude,

You're not going to believe this, but I, Lucy B. Parker, stood up to Rachel and Missy, my two ex-BFFs who dumped me last year. IN PERSON. It was beyond awesome. Sure, I was scared, but now I feel really great.

Well, I felt great. Then I got back to Dad's and had to listen to more talk about Ziggy. Even our alone time together at the Pioneer Valley flea market was spent talking about him. Mom says I should have had a Conversation-with-a-capital-C with him about the whole thing so we could discuss my feelings. But as far as I'm concerned, he's the adult, and therefore he should know better. Plus, I'm kind of sick of discussing my feelings.

Getting back to the Rachel/Missy thing for a second, though. It got me thinking more about Laurel's suggestion from the other day that I run for class president in the fall so I can do my part to end Mean People–ism and dork discrimination.

After the year I just had—with the move, and the new school, and the new family—I was looking forward to just finally relaxing, but I don't know ... maybe I should think more about it.

Mom just pulled up to pick me up for the trip back to New York, so I have to go. I'll let you know what I decide.

yours truly,

LUCY B. PARKER

Because there was a lot of traffic, I had six hours instead of four and a half to think about the running-for-president thing. By hour five, I still wasn't convinced. But after we stopped for gas and I went into the mini-mart and saw two teenage boys snickering as an old man had trouble grabbing a bag of potato chips off the display because his hand wouldn't stop shaking (I finally grabbed it for him), I realized Mean People weren't just in New York City. Or Northampton. They were *everywhere*. Laurel was right— the problem had to be stopped. And if I was a good person— and wanted to help my karma—I'd do my part to help.

As we got back into the car, I got excited that I'd finally have something exciting to share at our family dinner that night. When you live with someone whose news is along the lines of "I've been invited to the president's daughter's birthday party" and "They want me to sing at the Grammys . . . for the third year in a row," things like "I got an 82 on my math quiz" and "I went to Claire's and bought a headband" are a little on the boring side.

After the World News segment of the dinner, which was the part where Alan handed out photocopies of the top news stories of the day from *The New York Times*, I cleared my throat. "I'm still not one hundred percent sure, but I'm THINKING of running for class president when school starts," I announced.

Except that's not what Mom, Alan, and Laurel heard. What they heard was "I'm TOTALLY, DEFINITELY running for class president when school starts." Then they totally freaked out—especially Laurel, who screamed so loud you would've thought she was auditioning for a horror movie.

"Oh Lucy! This is such fabulous news!" Alan said excitedly after we had all made sure we hadn't gone deaf. "This is going to look so great on your college applications—"

"College applications?" I asked, confused. "But I'm just going into seventh grade."

"Yes, but you can never start beefing up your extracurricular activities too early," he replied. "No Ivy League school is going to even *look* at you if they don't see that you're well rounded. Do they have a debate club at the Center?" he asked. "Colleges *love* debaters. And you'd be great at it. Or what about Model UN? That would be even better! But even if you don't get around to that, class president carries a lot of weight—"

"But I'm not sure yet that I'm definitely running," I corrected him. "I said I was *thinking* about it. School hasn't even started yet." I looked over at Mom. She was always going on about how Alan tended to get overexcited about things. She'd help me out here, right?

"Sweetie, I'm *so* glad to see you really getting involved in your new school!" she bubbled. "You know, all the books talk about how when girls hit a certain age, their self-esteem levels drop and that's when they begin to defer to men, which is something that they then spend their entire adulthood recovering from, but when you're class president, you'll be way ahead of the curve!"

What was she talking about? "But I didn't say I was doing it for *sure*," I said again. "I said I was *thinking* about it." I turned to Laurel. "Can you believe how they're so not listening to me?" I whispered. "Help me out here. *Please.*"

But she wasn't listening, either. Instead, she had grabbed for one of the many little pads of paper and pens that Alan insisted be kept around the apartment so that we could write down important things that shouldn't be forgotten. "Okay, the first thing we have to do is put together a calendar so that we can come up with a schedule," she announced as she scribbled away. "Luckily, Office Depot sent me one of those giant wall ones with my last order ... I guess they do that when you spend over five hundred dollars—" Laurel was majorly into organization.

"Wait a minute—" I said.

But she, like everyone else, continued to ignore me. "And then we're going to need a bunch of file folders," she went on. "Good thing I just got a new label maker. Because we'll need folders for stuff like POTENTIAL CAMPAIGN SLOGANS and MATERIAL FOR SPEECHES. Oh, and OUTFITS WORN WHILE CAMPAIGNING—you don't want to repeat yourself."

I looked down at my cat, Miss Piggy, who was in her usual position of lying near my feet in hopes of snagging some falling food. Which, because of my coordination issue, happened at least twice a meal. Although she didn't like me, the way she was purring so loud made me think that even *she* thought this campaign thing was a good idea.

Laurel put down the pen and grabbed my arm. "Omigod, I'm *so* excited you decided to take my advice and do this!" she squealed. "It's going to be so fun to be your campaign manager!"

I had never said anything about her being my *campaign manager*!

In fact, one of the things I had been thinking about during the ride home was that, if I *did* run (and I wasn't even sure of *that*), it was really important to me that Laurel's involvement be more on the bubble-letters-on-posters and baking side (she was really awesome at bubble letters, and her brownies were delicious), and NOT on the public Laurel-Moses-Superstar side. Because as much as I loved Laurel, if I was going to run, it needed to be as *me*, Lucy B. Parker.

Not Lucy-B.-Parker-Laurel-Moses's-Non-Famous-Frister.

As my family began to chatter about *my* campaign as if I wasn't even in the room—the one for the election I wasn't even sure I was going to be running in—I slumped down in my chair and sighed.

Why was this already beginning to feel like a big mistake?

Even though I still had another week before school started and I would have to officially decide whether or not to run, my family kept going on and on about it like it was a done deal. Sure, I was excited when Mom said that I could buy a bunch of new outfits for the campaign, but what if I didn't end up running? Would I still be able to keep the clothes?

Every two seconds Laurel was texting me with new ideas. Her latest one was that she'd come to school with me one day and help hand out pencils that said "Vote for Me—Lucy B.!" In fact, she had already found a site online that would make them really cheap. It was a good idea—or would be, if, you know, she wasn't the most famous girl in America. But she was, and that meant that the kids at school who took the pencils would be taking them not because they wanted a good reminder of who to vote for on election day, but because they wanted to meet Laurel.

I needed some advice. And because Dr. Maude wasn't getting back to me, I decided to go to the second-best advice giver I knew: Pete, my doorman. He hadn't finished college, but according to him, he had a Ph.D. in Life. Which, also according to him, was the best training a person could get.

"Okay, so if I'm hearing you correctly," he said after I was done telling him my problem, "what you're saying is that you don't want Laurel involved with your campaign."

"See, that's part of the problem!" I cried. "People keep talking about 'my' campaign, but I haven't even decided for sure that I'm going to do it!"

"Oh, you're doing it," Pete said, in his I'm-a-doorman-so-I-know-everything voice.

"How do you know?" I demanded.

He shrugged. "I'm a doorman. We know these things." As he gave one of his longer sighs, I plopped down on the couch next to his desk. Long sighs = lectures = you wanted to be comfortable while having to sit through them. "Look, Lucy—we all have our callings. Laurel? Hers is to entertain people around the world. Mine? Doorman," he explained. "Yours? To stick up for all the kids at your school who need to be stuck up for and show that Cristina Pollock twerp what's what."

"Yeah, well, what if I don't want to answer the call?" I asked. "What if I just let it go to voice mail?"

He shrugged. "It just keeps calling back until you do. "Believe me, I'm a doorman—"

"And you know about this stuff," I finished.

"And as for Laurel, she just wants to help," he went on. "You know, because she loves you and all that."

"So I'll let her help," I said. "But with things like ... I don't know ... making files. And baking. And labeling things. Not with signed autographed pictures of herself wearing a GOT LUCY B. PARKER AS YOUR PRESIDENT? T-shirt."

"Look, Lucy, I know you probably won't believe me when I say this, but I have a theory."

I looked at my watch. When Pete got into one of his theories, he could go on forever, which meant I might miss *It's Me or the Ferret* on Animal Planet.

"And the theory is this," he continued. "I think that if Laurel wasn't Laurel Moses, I think she'd be considered one of those ... whatchamacallits ... deeks."

"Huh?"

"Deeks. The thing you say people get discriminated against for."

"You mean *dork*?" I asked. "You think Laurel is a *dork*?"

He looked around the lobby. "Shh. Keep your voice down." Luckily, the only person there was Mr. Grossman and his basset hound, Snoopy, and I knew from trying to have a conversation with Mr. Grossman in the elevator about how cute Snoopy's long ears were that he was very hard of hearing. "No, I don't think Laurel is a dork.

But I think that if she was a regular girl going to regular school, some people might think she had some habits that were kind of . . . *deek*like."

"It's dork," I corrected again. Although *deek* was a good word. Sort of a combination of geek and dork. In fact, it was so good, maybe I could submit it to urbandictionary.com. I had already written them to see if I could get overlistening and bloversharing put in there, but hadn't heard back yet. "You mean the way she loves office supply catalogs almost as much as fashion magazines?" I asked.

He nodded.

"And the way that she separates all her food on her plate and none of the different piles can touch and then she takes one bite from one, and then one from another?"

"Yeah. That kind of stuff," he replied. "Now me, I have no problem with that stuff, but some people, you know, they might think that's a little strange."

Some people? She was my best friend and frister, and *I* thought it was strange. But I could see what Pete was getting at.

"So you winning this election," Pete went on, "is not just about you giving a voice to the kids at school. It's about *her*, too."

I shrugged. "I guess."

"Let me put it this way: What if, instead of being your famous frister, she was just your regular frister, and

Mean People like Cristina were teasing her, what would you do?" Pete asked.

"That's easy. I'd stick up for her," I replied.

He nodded. "So just think of the kids at school as being your fristers and frothers. And if she wants to help because, whether she realizes it or not, this is kind of about her, too, why not let her? It's what happens *after* you win that's important."

I sighed. "Yeah. I see what you mean."

"Good. So you'll do it?" he asked excitedly.

"I don't know. I have to discuss it with my advisers," I said.

Meaning Beatrice and Alice. The good news was that because they knew what Cristina was capable of, they'd agree that the idea of my running was a setup for a seriously miserable school year.

On the way to the elevator I texted them about it. By the time I got back up to my apartment on the twenty-first floor, they had both responded. In all caps Alice had written OMG OMG OMG I LOVE LOVE LOVE THAT IDEA!!!!!!! Although I found the way she used nine million exclamation marks annoying, it was better than having to listen to her squeal. Beatrice's "Huh. I like it" meant she also thought it was a good idea. Although right after that, she wrote that she'd be sure to give a really awesome speech at my funeral if, for some reason,

I ended up mysteriously dying during the campaign thanks to Cristina.

What I ended up deciding was that I had to get through the first day of school first. See what Cristina was like. Maybe spending the entire summer at her family's house on Martha's Vineyard had somehow made her a nice person. I know if *I* had gotten to do that rather than going to museums with Mom, I'd be in a good mood. But I wasn't making any decisions about the campaign until then.

Except for one. The time had come to tell Laurel to cut it out with the posters and the binders and the T-shirts and the mugs. I sat in my room, sifting through all my possible first-day-of-school outfits from the ginormous lump of clothes on my bed, and tried to figure out how to best approach the situation with Laurel. In the nicest way possible, I was going to have to say, "Listen, Laurel, as grateful as I am that you want to help, I need you to butt out already."

Just as I was about to go to her room to do it, she burst into mine.

"You're not going to believe what I just did!" she squealed.

"Laurel, look, I'm super-thankful for all your help with the campaign, and don't take this the wrong way, but I really need you to stop helping," I blurted nervously. "Because if I end up doing this, then I want to do it as Lucy-B.-Parker-myself rather than

Lucy-B.-Parker-Laurel-Moses's-little-frister, okay?" I waited for more blurting to come out of my mouth, but nothing happened. Okay, so that wasn't too bad. I hadn't said anything particularly mean. What a relief. "See, the thing of it, you're just *too famous to help*," I blurted.

Uh-oh. From the way her eyes got all teary, and her bottom lip started to move back and forth like there was a Mexican jumping bean sewn into it, that part may have been on the mean side.

"Laurel, that's not what I meant," I quickly said. "I'm sorry. I didn't mean it to come out like that—" Oh, this was really not good. Stupid bloversharing.

"No, I get it," she said with a little sniffle. Great. Sniffling was just two seconds away from full-blown crying. And up until this election stuff we had been getting along so well lately. "It's just that . . . I just wish you had said something a little earlier!" she wailed as she burst into tears.

I could understand being upset, but bursting into tears? That seemed a little on the dramatic side. Even if you were an actress.

"Because after what I'm about to tell you," she hiccupped, "you're probably not going to be happy."

Uh-oh. I didn't like the sound of this. "Like how *not* happy are we talking about?" I asked.

"Like very, very, VERY not happy," she confessed. "See, I did something that, when I think about it, I probably should've run by you first—"

Before she could go on, my phone and e-mail blinged at the same exact time. I looked at my phone. *I CAN'T BELIEVE YOU WENT AHEAD AND ANNOUNCED YOUR CAMPAIGN!!!!* read a text from Beatrice. *I THOUGHT WE HAD DECIDED YOU WERE GOING TO WAIT!!*

Oh no.

"See, what I wanted to tell you—" she went on.

Just then, from over on my desk, my laptop blinged again. And again. And *again*.

Unlike Laurel, who sometimes got two hundred e-mails a day, I was lucky if I broke ten. And most of them were from bakeries around New York City because I was on all the mailing lists. I walked over to my desk and clicked on my in-box. It was filled with notifications of comments on my Facebook page. When I logged in and saw what was going on, my legs got so rubbery I had to grab on to my desk chair.

"How did people find out I was thinking of running against Cristina?! School hasn't even STARTED!" I cried. I read some more. "Wait a minute—they think I'm DEFINITELY running!"

"Okay, well, the reason for that is because—" Laurel said nervously.

"I'm going to *kill* Alice!" I cried, clicking onto her page. "I knew I shouldn't have told her about this yet."

"Actually, I don't think Alice is the one you should be mad at ... See, what happened was—"

I scanned Alice's Facebook page. But instead of

a status update like "Alice is excited that her friend Lucy B. Parker is running for class president," she had one of her usual dumb status updates: "*Alice is bored.*" (She usually switched off among "Alice is bored," "Alice is hungry," and "Alice is excited for this week's episode of *Prom Queen Princesses.*") "Okay, *what* is going on here?" I cried. "If Alice didn't blab it, how did all these people find out about this?"

Laurel cringed as she took a deep breath. "I . . . kind of, sort of put it as my Facebook update," she blurted out.

"You WHAT?!" I yelled as I began to pace.

She nodded. "And . . . I tweeted about it."

I paced faster. Could this get any worse?

"And . . . I wrote a blog entry about it," she continued. "You know, about how you're going to fight to end dork discrimination and to get rid of Mean People."

Yes. Yes, it could get worse. I stopped pacing. "But Laurel—that wasn't your news to report!" I cried. "It was *mine!*"

"I'm just so proud of you!" she cried. "I guess I just wanted everyone to know what an amazing frister I have. I'd never have the guts to do something like this."

"And who says that *I* do?!" I demanded. "And, even more than that, what if I don't *want* to?" I asked. "What if I just want to have a school year where everything is normal for once? Where I'm just part of the crowd instead of the New Girl, or Period Girl, or a famous superstar's younger frister? Why can't I just be Lucy B. Parker?! Is that too much to ask?!"

"I was just trying to help," she said quietly.

"I'll tell you how you can help—by butting out!" I snapped.

She stood up and stomped toward the door. "Fine. I'll do that then," she snapped back.

"Good."

The second she was gone, I immediately felt bad. I knew she was trying to help, but I hadn't asked for help. And this was not *helping*.

I sat down on my bed to think. Maybe I was overreacting. Maybe it wasn't as big of a deal as I was making it out to be. Maybe Cristina would think the idea of me running against her was ... a good thing. You know, because no one else had even dared to do so for the last three years except for some boy from Singapore who knew nothing about the popularity food chain. (Needless to say, he lost. Badly.) Maybe I'd run, and if I won, after I gave my acceptance speech, I'd turn to Laurel and say "Boy, am I glad you talked me into running for president. This is the best thing that ever happened to me in my entire life!"

I walked over to my desk, and looked at my Facebook page again. Underneath the comments that said things like, "*Hey, Parker—haven't you heard that class president is Cristina Pollock's job?*" and "*You're either really brave ... or really stupid!,*" another one popped up.

From Cristina.

"You do realize war has just been declared, right?"

I could feel myself start to sweat.

Another comment popped up.

"And you are so dead."

Okay, I was right. I wasn't overreacting after all. It wasn't a big deal—it was a HUGE deal.

chapter 4

Dear Dr. Maude,

Sorry if there are any typos in this e-mail, but I'm writing it at 1:15 a.m. in the morning on my iTouch from underneath my covers.

Things are NOT good at the moment. It's kind of a long story, so I won't go into all of it now, but there are three main points to it. The first is that Laurel went ahead and told the entire world that I'm running against Cristina for class president.

The second is that since Cristina would be considered part of the entire world, that means she now knows. And she's not happy about it. Beatrice says it's a free country, and anyone can run for president. But she also says that I should make sure I don't delete Cristina's Facebook comments about how I'm going to regret this so that I have them as evidence in case anything mysterious happens to me, which is a trick she learned from the TV show *Law & Order*.

But the third—and most important—point is that after I found out about the Facebook Incident, I got really mad at Laurel. Like to the point where we haven't said a word to each other since then. Not at dinner. Or during Family TV

Time. We didn't even talk when she knocked on my door and threw that purple Indian-looking shirt of hers with the cool embroidery that I love so much at me because she had promised me I could wear it tomorrow on the first day of school. (BTW? As much as I want to, I'm not going to.)

I talked to Mom about the whole thing, and she says that I'm overreacting and that Laurel's just trying to help, but Dr. Maude, it's not just the Facebook Incident that's got me mad. It's ALL of it. It's the fact that I feel that no one bothers to listen to me. Do you think that's because I'm the youngest? Do ALL kids who are the youngest have it this bad?

I know you know that my big fear when Mom fell in love with Alan was that because Laurel is so famous, I'd totally disappear and stop being Lucy B. Parker and instead be Lucy-Laurel's-less-pretty-untalented-younger-stepsister. And you also know that, luckily, that didn't really end up happening. Well, that is, UNTIL NOW. Which is why I'm so upset.

I felt like Mom was all on Laurel's side. (Do you find that happens a lot? That a lot of the time parents are overly nice to the kid who is not their birth kid in order to make that kid like them more? Because that's sure been my experience.) So I called Dad to see what he had to say about the whole thing. Yeah, well, THAT was a HUGE mistake. As we were talking, I could hear the clicking of computer keys, and when I said, "Dad, are you typing on the computer instead of listening to this very important, very dramatic thing that happened to me this afternoon?" you know what he said? He said, "Uh, yes. Sorry about that, Lucy. I'll stop now. I was just looking at changing tables on the Babies R Us website. But now I'm going to give you my undivided attention."

As if I really WANTED it after that. And then my finger accidentally happened to push the End button on my phone. (Okay, fine, maybe not accidentally.)

This is all too much drama for me. I know some kids like drama (like, say, kids in the drama club), but I don't. As far as I'm concerned, I'm perfectly happy letting Laurel be the dramatic one in the family. Which makes sense, seeing that she's an actress and all.

I guess I should try and go to sleep now.

Wish me luck in not getting killed tomorrow.

yours truly,
LUCY B. PARKER

"Good morning, Miss Piggy," I said when I walked into the kitchen the next morning and found Laurel dividing the fruit from the nuts in her granola. "Miss Piggy, don't you just hate it when people don't accept your apology?" Once, when I was mad at Mom back in Northampton, I had spoken to her through Miss Piggy, and it had worked really well.

Laurel looked up and glared at me. "Miss Piggy, can you tell whoever just said that that texts do not count as official apologies? Especially if it's worded like the one I got last night."

I glared back. "Miss Piggy, I don't know about you, but I think that a text that says 'Fine. Maybe I could've handled that better but, still, you're totally the one who started all this' is a perfectly good apology. But I guess *some* people don't think that *they* did anything wrong to begin with."

"*Someone* already *said* she was sorry to *someone else's* face, Miss Piggy!" she cried. "But apparently, that person didn't think that was good enough. And then she had to go all Brianna Machado on her."

I gasped. "Miss Piggy, can you please tell the person who just said that that I am so not like Brianna!" Brianna Machado was this new character on Laurel's show who was her archrival and a total nightmare. She was always pitching fits and having meltdowns. You'd think viewers would hate her, but actually, they couldn't get enough of her, which didn't make Laurel all that happy. Especially because she said that Harlee Huntley, the actress who played her, was like that in real life, too.

Laurel just shrugged and went back to dividing up her granola.

"Okay, you know what, Miss Piggy?" I said. "Someone hereby takes back her kind-of, sort-of apology! And doesn't really care if someone else is mad at her or not."

I stomped out of the kitchen. When I got back to my

room and closed the door, I burst into tears. Laurel and I had had little fights before, but this was different.

This was *serious*.

"Look at it this way," Beatrice said brightly as we walked to school later on. "Instead of worrying about the election, now you can spend all your time worrying about whether your mom and Alan are going to have to split up!" As always, Beatrice was wearing her usual uniform of all black—this time a black miniskirt, a short-sleeved button-down shirt, and black Converses. (I got to take credit for getting her into sneakers.) Plus, she had a jet-black bob, which made her even more New York-y-looking.

I, on the other hand, was wearing a lilac minidress with brown cowboy boots and a red beret. I figured all the color might make me seem braver than I actually felt. Not to mention take away some of the sadness about my fight with Laurel. "What? Who said anything about their splitting up?" I asked nervously.

She shrugged. "Well, if things are as bad as you say they are between you and Laurel—"

"We had a fight!" I cried. "People fight all the time. It's part of being in a family."

She shrugged again. "Okay. Forget I said anything."

But Beatrice's "Forget I said anything" did not mean "Forget I said anything." What it meant was, "You can sit there and try to fool yourself for as long as you want, but what just happened"—whatever "it" happened to be—"is not good."

"It'll be fine," I said with a lot more confidence than I actually felt. "We'll make up." Or we wouldn't, and Mom and Alan would decide to send me off to boarding school because what would come out is that they loved Laurel more than me.

Beatrice shrugged again. "Okay. Whatever you say."

That was another phrase that meant something else. In this case it meant, "Ha—you are so fooling yourself with that one."

"Let's talk about the election," I said quickly as we reached Hakim and his doughnut cart on Broadway and Eighty-sixth. One of my favorite things about New York City was that there was a food cart on every street corner. Some sold fruit; some sold hot dogs; and some— my favorite ones—sold doughnuts.

I paid for a powdered-sugar doughnut and turned to Beatrice. (After the run-in with Laurel in the kitchen, I had been forced to leave the house without breakfast.) "I was thinking that after we get the posters done, I'll order some buttons—maybe some pencils, too—we'll bake some cookies, and that will be that."

"What do you meant 'that will be that'?" she asked.

I shrugged. "Back in Northampton, that's how the elections are done. Buttons. Pencils. Cookies. Done."

She shook her head. "Yeah, well, you're not in

Northampton anymore," she said. As if the tall buildings, honking, yellow cabs, and women wearing high heels didn't give *that* away. "Here in New York, school elections are a lot different."

She opened her *J'AIME PARIS* book bag (*J'aime* is French for "I love"—Beatrice wants to live there when she grows up) and took out a folder that was labeled OPERATION ELECTION. As soon as I saw it, I couldn't help getting a little sad. File folders = Laurel. Who I wasn't talking to at the moment and therefore couldn't text *What have I gotten myself into?!*

She handed me a typed piece of paper. "Things to Do for Operation Election Over the Next Three Weeks," I read aloud. "Put name on sign-up sheet. Prepare 'What I'd Do If I Were Elected President' speech." I turned to her. "Wait a minute—a speech?" I cried. "No one said anything about public speaking! I'm awful at it. Every time I have to do it, I end up bloversharing!"

"Of course you have to give a speech," she replied. "Haven't you ever seen the news? That's pretty much all presidents *do*."

"Start meeting with as many Have-Nots as possible to hear their concerns," I continued reading. I looked up at her again. "What's a Have-Not?"

"That's what I thought we could call the dork population," Beatrice explained. "Because it sounds nicer. And then we could call Cristina Pollock and the popular crowd the Haves. So it would be the Haves versus the Have-Nots."

Huh. That *was* catchy. So catchy that it almost but not quite made me excited to be running. I looked back at the page. "Set up website, complete with shopping cart so we can sell T-shirts and hats. Set up Facebook fan page and Twitter account. Put together video—" I looked up again. "Video?"

"Every candidate can do a video." She handed me a packet of papers with tons of tiny print. "See, because no one's ever had the guts to run against Cristina before, except that kid from Singapore, there's never been a real campaign part of the election. But the election rules are on the school website, so I downloaded them." She pointed to a piece of paper. "See—right there. *'Candidates are allowed to make videos, provided they are not used to say mean things about other candidates. Otherwise, first said candidate will be promptly disqualified from the race.'*"

"But I hate being filmed," I said nervously. "I get all tongue-tied and sweaty. Sometimes I get nervous on Skype with Connor, and even Dad." Not like I'd have to worry about that anymore. Dad would be so busy looking at the Babies R Us website he wouldn't even be paying attention.

"Look, Lucy, do you want to win this thing or not?" Beatrice asked. "Because if you do, you're going to have to go all out."

Did I want to *win*? I didn't even want to *run*. Right?

I looked down at the list, which seemed to go on and on. "Prepare wrap-up speech," I read. "Two speeches?

That's just wrong. We didn't even have to give two speeches during the oral presentations part of English last year. We only had to give one."

"If you win, you're going to have to do a lot of public speaking," she replied. "That's what happens when you're famous. I mean, look at Laurel."

Great. After a Laurel-free brain for the last few minutes, now she popped back in and I had to think about her and how much I missed her. Even if I did think that the way she was handling this whole thing was really stupid.

"But I don't *want* to be famous," I said. "I like being *un*famous." I hadn't thought about all that. I mean, if I were president, I wouldn't be invisible anymore. Which meant that if I was having a particularly bad hair or zit day, people would totally see it.

I sighed. Forget about spending my afternoons for the next month until the election watching Dr. Maude and *telenovelas* with Rose. This campaign thing was going to be a full-time job. And I wasn't even getting paid for it.

To anyone else, it would've looked like the three girls standing in the lobby of the Center for Creative Learning were there to greet people. Dressed in identical pink miniskirts, white tank tops, and black cardigans, all lined up in a row with their hands on their hips, they looked like an ad for pretty, rich girls with pimple-free skin. But I knew better. They were Cristina Pollock, Tweedle Dee (her BFF Chloe) and Tweedle Dumber (her other BFF Marni). And I knew they weren't there to greet me. Especially when, as we got closer, I saw the very unfriendly, ungreeter-like scowls on their face.

And especially when a tall skinny blonde girl whose arms and legs were so long that she looked like a piece of human spaghetti came running up to us. "I hate to be the one to tell you this, Lucy, but Cristina sooooo wants to kill you!" she yelled through her mouthful of braces.

I cringed. Alice couldn't help the fact that she was deaf in one ear, but the way she yelled things could be very embarrassing.

"*Merci* for the breaking-news special report, Alice," said Beatrice. "Lucy already knows that."

I looked at her. Yes, I did already know that. But as my BFF, could she at least *pretend* that my life wasn't going to end in five minutes?

"I can't believe my entire seventh-grade experience is going to be over before I even make it to homeroom," I moaned.

"It'll be fine," Beatrice promised me. "Just keep walking." It was pretty amazing to me how Beatrice wasn't the least bit scared of Cristina. She said that was because when you've seen someone in her underwear during sleepovers back from the days you used to be BFFs with her, it takes away any of the scary stuff. "Alice, get on the other side of Lucy and let's all link arms," she said. "That way we'll act as bodyguards in case there's anyone hiding in the shadows waiting to try anything funny."

I turned to her. "Okay, you really need to stop watching those detective shows," I said. "Because that stuff is *not* helping."

"Hello, *Cristina*," Beatrice harrumphed as Team Have-Not made our human chain stop in front of the Haves.

"*Beatrice*," Cristina harrumphed back. "You're looking as dead as ever."

Tweedle Dee and Tweedle Dumber giggled, while Beatrice's pale white skin got all blotchy with embarrassment.

This was why Cristina needed to be stopped—because of this kind of meanness.

I squeezed Beatrice's arm in mine. As her blotches faded, Beatrice stood up a little taller. Which, because she was on the short side, didn't make that much of a difference. "I was hoping with the new school year I wouldn't have to listen to *that* again," Beatrice said. "But I guess you were too busy copying Laurel Moses's outfit and haircut to come up with original insults. Or original outfits."

So *that's* why Cristina's (and Tweedle Dee's, and Tweedle Dumber's) outfit looked familiar! It was the same one that Laurel had worn in the most recent episode of *Madison*. And Beatrice was right—Cristina's long blonde hair was cut in the same bangs-and-long-layers way.

Except Laurel was like a bajillion times prettier than Cristina. Probably because she was so much nicer. Well, when she wasn't busy turning down my apology.

Most people, if they got busted on something like that, would've turned red, too. But not Cristina. "So Lucy, you're really going to do this?" she asked.

I gave a maybe, I'm-not-sure, why-not shrug.

She leaned in. "Just remember—if you put your name on that sign-up sheet at the end of the day, you are *so* going to regret it," she hissed before turning around on her heel so fast that her hair fanned out like Laurel's did in the *Gee Your Hair Smells Awesome* shampoo commercial. It totally wasn't fair that someone so mean had such pretty hair.

I already *did* regret it. And I hadn't even signed up yet.

"If you win, I want to be in charge of the social stuff, okay?" Alice said later as we sat at our lunch table in Alaska. That's what Beatrice called it because, according to her Googling, that was the farthest point north in the United States. A lot of the Have-Nots sat in the same area of the cafeteria. Mostly the drama club geeks, and the band geeks, and the normal geeks like us. In Hawaii, which was the farthest point south, were the gamers. Everyone tried to stay away from them, because of the B.O. factor.

As for Cristina Pollock, her table was in Lebanon, Kansas, which was smack in the middle of the country.

"If I'm in charge of the social stuff, I can plan a bunch of dances." Alice said.

"Dances? Who said anything about dances?" I asked. If anything, if I were elected I'd try to get *rid* of the dances at school—especially the Sadie Hawkins one. That was when the girls had to ask the boys. Because I was *not* going to have to ask a boy to a dance. Luckily our grade wasn't part of it, but I was going to try to get rid of it entirely so I wouldn't have to deal with it when I was old enough to go.

I took out my latest notebook—*Important Things to Remember to Do If I Am Elected President*—from my tote bag. "*Remember to GET RID of Sadie Hawkins Dance!!!!*" I wrote.

"And I want to be in charge of rewriting the school handbook," Beatrice said. "Like how to behave and what's considered rude and bad manners and stuff like that."

I loved Beatrice, but she could be what Mom sometimes called Alan when I was overlistening to her on the phone with Deanna: a "total control freak." "I don't think the students are in charge of the handbook," I replied. "I think Dr. Rem-Wall writes it." That was short for "Remington-Wallace," our principal.

She shrugged. "Well, the students *should* get to write it," she said. "Like, for instance, *me*."

"Guys, I haven't even officially signed up yet, let alone

won," I reminded them. I turned to Malia Nicolato, a tall girl with long, dark, curly hair who had joined our lunch table threesome and turned it into a foursome. Malia was the new New Girl at the Center. Because I had been the New Girl last spring, I totally understood how she felt.

Which is why I had passed her a note asking if she wanted to sit with us at lunch, as my new teacher Mr. Eglington (aka Eagle Eye) went on and on about everything we were going to cover in English this year. I knew from experience that the kids at the Center never got the memo that asking New Kids to sit with you at lunch gave you good karma. I had spent my first two lunches last spring in the bathroom, and it had *not been* fun.

"Malia, would you like to be part of my campaign for president?" I asked shyly. "If I win—I mean, I probably won't, but if I do—you can be in charge of something, too." Granted I had known Malia for only fifteen minutes, so for all I knew she could be completely weird, but it's not like anyone else was running up asking to be part of my administration.

She shrugged. "Sure. As long as I don't have to do anything exercise- or math-related."

I smiled. I knew there was a reason I liked her right away. "Nope. None of that stuff will be involved. In fact, I was thinking that one of my campaign promises will be to try and get rid of gym class." I would have liked to try to get rid of math, too, but I doubted the school would go for that.

"That's a good one," Beatrice agreed. "Most Have-Nots aren't fans of physical exercise." She pointed at a table of particularly icky gamers over in Hawaii. "They tend to sweat enough without it."

Alice turned to Malia. "Lucy's going to run against Cristina Pollock—can you believe that?!"

"Who's Cristina Pollock?"

Alice pointed over to where Cristina was walking around to different tables in Hawaii and sampling whatever she wanted from kids' lunches while they sat there paralyzed. Some kids—like Justin Wagner—were so scared of her that they literally slid down and hid under the table as she got closer. "See that really pretty blonde girl?" Alice asked. "The one who looks just like Laurel Moses? That one."

I rolled my eyes. "I keep telling you, Alice," I said, "other than the haircut, they really don't look anything alike."

Alice turned to Malia. "If anyone would know what Laurel looks like, it's Lucy," she said. "They're fristers." So much for not being reminded of Laurel. And the fact that we were in a ginormous fight.

"What's a frister?" Malia asked.

"It's a combination of friend and sister," I explained. "I thought it was a nicer word than 'stepsister.' You know, because when people think of stepsister, they think of girls who don't really like each other and fight all the time. Also, our parents aren't married yet."

"Kind of like how you and Laurel are fighting now," Beatrice said.

"Okay, changing the subject," I said.

"Ohhh. *That* girl. She had some boy put an uncapped red marker on your seat when you went to the bathroom in English," she said.

"She did?! I didn't know that!" I cried.

"That's because I reached over and took it off before you came back." She smiled.

I smiled, too. Okay, seeing that she had saved me from severe embarrassment on account of the fact that if I had sat on it, it totally would've made it look like I had gotten my period, we were officially friends.

"So what you're saying is that Cristina is the Chiara Conticchio of the school," Malia said.

"Who's Chiara Conticchio?" Alice asked, confused.

"The most popular girl back at my school in Milan." Malia had spent the last two years in Milan because her father, who was a famous painter, was Italian and needed to go back to his homeland for inspiration ("Well, that, and the fact that the rent-stabilized building we lived in went condo and my parents couldn't afford to buy our apartment.")

Chiara Conticchio. That totally sounded like a Mean Girl's name. "They have Mean Girls in Italy, too?" Alice asked.

"Oh yeah. Tons of them. And when you're being bullied in Italian, it sounds even worse than it does in English."

"That's why Lucy's running for class president," Alice said. "To stop Mean People–ism and dork discrimination."

"Wow. That's great," Malia said, impressed. "I was discriminated against up until last year because of my weight."

I looked at her, confused. "But you're so skinny," I said.

"And tall," Beatrice sighed.

"That's because I grew six inches in fifth grade," Malia explained. "Before that I was about your height and I was really fat. Kids would call me all sorts of names."

"But now you look like a *model*," Alice said.

"And your hair is so curly without being frizzy," Beatrice sighed as she ran her hand through her so-straight-it-tended-to-just-lie-there hair.

She shrugged. "I may look different *now*, but I'm still a dork," she said. "I mean, how many people do you know who know all the songs from *Middle School Musical* by heart?"

Alice gasped. "I do! I do!"

Beatrice and I looked at each other. If she started singing "Gym Class Blues" right then and there, *I* was going to crawl underneath the table like Justin.

But that was the difference between Cristina and me. While I may have been embarrassed about my friend and her dorklike behavior, I wouldn't be mean and say something about it because that would hurt Alice's feelings. But Cristina—not only would she have said something, but she would've teased her about it for months. And probably given her some sort of nickname because of it to boot.

We went back to talking about the best way to organize the campaign stuff. And I went back to missing Laurel, because next to being a superstar and the Most Beautiful Teen in the World, organization was her specialty. How was I going to get through this thing without her?

I mean, I still didn't want her involved because even if she didn't intend to, she'd end up taking over the whole thing in her take-over-type way. But it would be weird to not have her around for this. It was kind of like . . . peanut butter without jelly. Or hot cocoa without marshmallows. Or sliced bananas without maple syrup.

Just then Jacqueline Mercier walked up to our table. Although not a dorky picked-last-for-volleyball-in-gym kind of Have-Not, she *was* a sci-fi-and-fantasy-reading Have-Not. "Hey, Lucy? Are you still keeping that crush log?" she asked.

As I nodded, Beatrice turned to Malia and explained. "Lucy keeps this log where all the girls can put down their crushes."

"You mean all three: local, long-distance/vacation, and celebrity?" Malia asked. "What an awesome idea."

I looked at her. "Are you telling me people in *Italy* know about the three-crush rule, too?"

She nodded. I couldn't believe it was an international thing.

"She also keeps a period log," Alice added.

"You can put me in that one as August 5, nine forty a.m.," Jacqueline said.

I reached into my bag for both logs. "You're so lucky," Alice sighed. "I really hope I don't have to wait until eighth grade until my name gets in there."

"Tell me about it," I mumbled as I wrote down Jacqueline's information in the period one. When I was done, I grabbed the crush log. "So who are your three?"

She fired off some names, but then quickly changed her mind, which meant I had to do some erasing. And then some more names. And more erasing. Until the paper actually ripped.

How was it that all these people could come up with three crushes and I couldn't even come up with one? "Look," I finally said. "Lunch is about over, so why don't you e-mail me them when you have it figured out and I'll put them in then," I said.

"Okay." She looked around to make sure no one was listening. "Oh, and I just want you to know—you can definitely count on my vote," she said in a low voice. "Someone needs to stop Cristina Pollock. And the fact that you're going to try means you're either *really* brave or *really* stupid. So good luck."

As she walked away, I looked at my friends. "Let's hope it's the first one?"

After lunch, Dr. Rem-Wall gave a reminder announcement that the sign-up sheet for elections would be up by the end of the day. Getting through the rest of the afternoon was next to impossible, especially because whenever I glanced over at Cristina, she was giving me the evil eye. It was a good thing I didn't believe in voodoo like Rose did, or else I would've been sure that she was putting some sort of curse on me. However, I was so nervous that I went to the bathroom no less than three times to check to see if I had gotten my period. Marissa said that anxiety was known to bring it on. I would've gone more if Mr. Eagle Eye hadn't said—in front of the entire class during social studies—"Lucy Parker, I'm sorry, but no one has to go to the bathroom that much. Now please sit down."

By the time the last bell rang, I was a wreck. And the fact that, as Beatrice dragged me down the hall while Alice and Malia pushed me from behind, I saw that the entire seventh grade was gathered around the sign-up sheet next to the gym didn't help. Cristina was standing right next to it, her arms crossed, with Tweedle Dee and Tweedle Dumber on either side of her.

In the vice president and secretary columns, a bunch of names were printed, but in the president column there was only one: Cristina Pollock.

"You're sure you want to do this?" Cristina demanded.

I opened my mouth to speak, but nothing came out. Great. If this was how it was going to be for the entire election, I was in big trouble.

"Yes. She's sure," Beatrice said. Maybe I could just get her to speak for me during this whole thing. Including the speeches part. *Especially* the speeches.

Cristina shrugged. She glared at me with a narrowed-eye Mean Girl look. "Don't say I didn't warn you, Parker."

I gave her my best narrowed-eye Mean Girl look back. Which, because I didn't have a lot of experience giving them, wasn't very good. "Okay. I won't."

Beatrice shoved a pen toward me. "Lucy, just put your name down, and let's get out of here."

"Okay, but I have to get my lucky pen!" I cried, going through my bag. I wasn't taking any chances. Finally, I found it—my purple ink, extra-fine-point one. I uncapped it and then got really sad because Laurel had bought it for me at her favorite stationery store up in Morningside Heights.

Beatrice turned to Alice. "All set with the video?"

She nodded as she aimed her flip camera toward me. She was going to be Team Have-Not's official video person. "Wait. There's no picture," she said, confused.

Malia leaned over. "I think it might work if you turned it on." On the other hand, maybe we were going to have to rethink that "official video person" thing.

Alice hit the button. "Okay, we're ready!" Alice yelled. "And . . . ACTION!"

Because my cursive wasn't that great, I made sure to go as slow as possible. The last thing I wanted was to somehow get disqualified because no one could read my name.

"Lucy, can you move a little to the right?" Alice called out.

As I did, my hand slipped (my coordination problems got a lot worse when I was nervous), so instead of *Lucy*, it looked like my name was *Lucp*. "Does anyone have any Wite-Out?" I called out. I tried not to get too sad as I thought about how if Laurel had been here, she would've had some with her.

"I do!" called out Martin Sage, who was almost as organized as Laurel.

After I fixed it, I began to write again. Until Alice dropped the camera. And it skidded across the floor and hit the wall so hard that the battery popped out.

Beatrice shook her head and sighed.

"It's okay," Malia said. "I'll just take a picture with my iPhone. I'll even use the Hipstamatic app so it looks really cool."

This time I made it through my entire name without messing up. I even made the period after the B in the shape of a star that actually looked like a star.

"Uh-oh," Malia said as she looked at her iPhone. "I didn't wait for it to save. Can you pretend you're signing again?"

Cristina walked up and peered at my name. "Well, it's official. You really *are* crazy." She turned toward the crowd. "For anyone who's interested, we're going to be handing out Vote-for-Cristina-Pollock fudgesicles in the gym!"

As a stampede started, I had to press myself up against the wall in order not to be knocked over. At the moment I kind of wished I wasn't running. All the nervousness about what I had just officially gotten myself into had suddenly made me really hungry, and I really liked fudgesicles.

chapter 5

Dear Dr. Maude,

You know how I told you how Laurel and I got in a fight? Well, it's three days later, and we're STILL in a fight. And a person doesn't have to be a famous psychologist like you to know that three days + no talking = BAD NEWS. Actually, that's not entirely true. We are talking a little bit—but it's stuff like, "Miss Piggy, can you ask Lucy to pass the ketchup, please?" and "Miss Piggy, please tell Laurel that her cereal bowl is on my side of the table."

If Mom and Alan were here, I'm sure that they would call an Emergency Parker-Moses Family Meeting and make us make up, but they decided to take a few days of QT, so they're at some fancy hotel in Connecticut. Probably doing it, because according to Marissa, that's what adults go to hotels to do. Which is so gross I can't even think about it.

So because of that, Rose is watching us. And because she doesn't really watch us, but instead watches a lot of TV, I don't think she notices that we're not talking.

The problem is, I really miss Laurel. And I feel like if I ever needed her, it's now, because of the campaign. Because the truth is, I'm really scared about it (especially the having-to-give-a-speech part). As cheesy as some of her pep talks can be because she tends to repeat stuff that has happened in Very Special episodes of her series, they also make me feel better.

In fact, I was all set to apologize to her last night— EVEN THOUGH I ALREADY DID in a text, although she says it wasn't a real apology. But when I got to her room, although her door was closed almost all the way, because of my extra-fantastic hearing, I just HAPPENED to hear her on the phone with Maya, her makeup artist. And because my leg was bothering me, which made it so it took me sort of a long time to walk away, I just HAPPENED to overlisten and hear her say that the way I was acting was "very immature."

First of all, that's so not true, and secondly, it's not like she's an adult or anything. I mean, she's only two years, three months, and six days older than me. Well, obviously I didn't end up apologizing because of that. And it's not even like I could say, "You know, I would've apologized, but then I heard you say I was immature," because then she'd know that I was overlistening and someone as quote-unquote MATURE as she is wouldn't understand the whole overlistening thing.

Do you have any advice for me as to how to make up with someone even if you think that you didn't do anything wrong and they should be the one to apologize to YOU?

yours truly,
LUCY B. PARKER

P.S. When you write back, if you could also give me some pointers on how to write a great speech, that would be very helpful, too.

"Okay, before we begin our Team Have-Not brainstorming session," I announced the next afternoon after school, "I just want to remind everyone"—at that, I looked at Alice—"that there's no bringing up You-Know-Who."

The brainstorming sessions would have taken place in my bedroom, but because Mom and Alan were out of town, we were in the kitchen chowing down on all the junk food we had bought with some of the campaign funds, aka my allowance.

"You mean Laurel, right?" Alice asked.

I sighed. "Yes, Alice. That's who You-Know-Who would be." Who, at that moment, was in her bedroom with the door closed, which was pretty much how it had been since our fight, other than that one time she had forgotten to close it so I overlistened and heard her call me immature.

She nodded. "Okay. Got it."

"So has anyone come up with any brilliant ideas since yesterday?" I asked as I rolled the sides of my ice cream sandwich in Fruity Pebbles.

Alice stopped pouring Hershey's chocolate syrup on her mini marshmallows. (Beatrice had been worried that spending part of our campaign funds on junk food was a bad idea, but I totally disagreed. Especially because it was my money. I mean, how could a person think well if all she had in her stomach was something healthy, like an apple?) Alice's hand shot up. "Oh! Oh! I have one!"

"Is this one as good as the one you had yesterday when you said that Lucy should walk around wearing deer antlers and handing out buttons that say, '*Dare to Be Different—Vote for Lucy B. Parker*'?" Beatrice asked as she gnawed at the white part of a double-stuffed Oreo with her teeth.

"What was wrong with that one?" Alice asked, hurt.

Beatrice rolled her eyes. "Because *deer* and *dare* are not the same word, Alice."

Alice shrugged. "They're close. The both have *d*'s and *e*'s in them."

"Sorry, but there will be no wearing of antlers or any other kind of animal ears," I announced as I finished erasing the whiteboard from yesterday's campaign slogan brainstorming session. Unfortunately, it hadn't been very brainstormy, because at the end of the day, we all decided that "Lucy B. Parker for President" wasn't all that creative.

Malia turned to Alice and smiled. "So what's your new brilliant idea?" She really was one of the nicest people I had ever met. It may have been because of the Italy thing, because back when Laurel and I were still friends, she had said Italians were the nicest people in the world.

"Okay. So the idea is . . . during your campaign speech, you announce that anyone who votes for you will get to be an extra on Laurel's TV show!" she said excitedly.

The three of us looked at one another. If this were a reading comprehension test, Alice so would have failed. "Okay, that's not going to work," I replied. "See, (a) you just mentioned You-Know-Who again," I explained. "And (b) before I even agreed to go through with this, I said that I'd only do it if we didn't play the whole my-frister-is-a-superstar card."

"Oh. Well, when you said that, it probably went into my left ear," she said, "which is why I didn't hear it."

"It was in a text," I replied. "And you wrote back: *'ok, but u'd totally win with that!'*"

"Fine, so I remember!" she cried. "It's just that it's such a super-awesome idea. Plus, this wouldn't be Laurel helping with the campaign. This would be Laurel helping *after* the campaign."

I stood up and walked around so that I was facing her right ear. "I'll say it again," I said. "I don't want You-Know-Who helping out with the campaign." I reached for my election notebook and a pen. "Now, let's talk about the speech. I was thinking that starting with 'Good afternoon, my fellow students. My name is Lucy B. Parker' might be a really good way to go."

"Beatrice, you might want to tell *someone* that 'My fellow students, good afternoon' flows better" came a voice from the end of the kitchen.

I looked up to see Laurel standing there with her arms crossed. "Beatrice, can you please tell the person who just said that that (a) I happen to think that 'Good afternoon, my fellow students' flows just fine, thankyouverymuch," I replied. "And (b) if she bothered to look at the sign-up sheet in the hall, she'd see that I had reserved this room until five." As soon as Mom and Alan left, Laurel had put up a sheet where we could reserve different rooms in the house so that we wouldn't run into each other.

"Well, I happen to be thirsty," Laurel said all huffily as she marched to the fridge and took out a bottle of water. Wait—because she had said that directly to me, did that mean she was talking to me again? And if so, did that mean we had made up even though there hadn't been an official apology?

This fighting business was very confusing.

Once she had the water, instead of going back to her room, she poured it into a glass and continued to stand there. "What?" she asked as we all stared at her.

"Um, we're in a campaign meeting?" I said.

"Oh right. Sorry. I should go, then," she said. "Seeing that *someone* doesn't want my help." I guess we weren't talking again after all. She pointed at the mess of papers that we had strewn across the kitchen table, some of them covered with smears of chocolate and glass ring stains. "Even though, from the looks of it, I'm not sure how anyone can get anything done when they're so . . . *unorganized.*"

"Okay, (a) that person will have you know that this may look like a mess, but it's an organized one," I replied. "And (b) I—I mean that person—I mean—" This whole talking-to-each-other-but-not-exactly thing was driving me crazy. "Anyway, we're doing just fine here."

"Fine," she said, stomping out. "I know when I'm not wanted," she announced over her shoulder.

"I never said you weren't wanted!" I yelled after her. "That's putting words in my mouth, which, if you look at the Official Parker-Moses Family Rule Book, you'll see is not allowed, according to rule number 22!" I turned to my friends. "Did you hear me say she wasn't wanted?"

They shrugged. "Maybe those exact words didn't come out of your mouth," Malia said. "But it *does* kind of seem like that."

"Well, that's not true," I replied. "If she just apologized, I'd be happy to have her help," I said. "But in a regular-friend way—not in a superstar kind of way."

"Why should I apologize again when I already apologized once?!" came Laurel's voice from behind the door.

"Okay, (a) stop overlistening," I yelled, "and (b) I already apologized once, too, so we're even!"

"That text was not an apology!" she yelled back.

Beatrice got up and started gathering up her stuff.

"Where are you going?" I asked.

"If you guys are just going to spend all your time fighting like this, I'm going to go home and watch TV. We're not getting anything done."

As Alice and Malia began to pack up as well, I sighed. Unfortunately, she was right. And we had *a lot* to do.

Luckily, after that, Laurel's shooting schedule got super-busy, so most nights I was already sleeping by the time she got home, and she was still sleeping by the time I left for school. That gave me plenty of time to practice my speech aloud without worrying that she was standing on the other side of the door overlistening and giving me all sorts of pointers that I hadn't asked her for.

Even though, because of all her appearances at the Emmys, the Grammys, and the MTV Movie Awards, she was an awesome speech giver and probably could have helped me write a great one. Still, when you practice a speech in the mirror, it's not like you're going to get very good feedback from the person looking out at you. So when Dad called one afternoon, I asked him if he'd listen and give me feedback.

"Sure, honey, I'd love to," he said.

"Great. But can I ask you a favor first?"

"I already know what you're going to say," he said. "And the answer is, of course I'll be honest even though you're my daughter."

"Actually, I was going to ask if you could turn off that sloshing-water CD," I said. "So I don't have to stop and go to the bathroom in the middle."

Once that was taken care of, he listened while I gave my speech. Because I couldn't see him, I had no idea if he was also thumbing through baby books or Babies R Us flyers or anything like that, but at least I couldn't hear him typing. "So what'd you think?" I asked when I was done.

"I thought it was just great, honey," he replied.

"Really? You did?"

"Absolutely. And it got me thinking—"

"That 'Good afternoon, my fellow students' sounds a lot better than 'My fellow students, good afternoon'?" I asked hopefully.

"No. I was thinking that maybe that Future Young Leaders of America for Toddlers workshop I saw advertised at the coffee shop the other day might not be such a bad thing for Ziggy to check out," he replied.

When did zombies come in and body snatch my real father and replace him with this guy, and just how could I get my real dad back? "Dad!"

"What?"

"You always said you couldn't stand those people!"

"What people?"

"The people who put their kids in classes when they can't even walk yet, and try and make it so they're geniuses with that baby-classical-music stuff!" I cried. "And now it's like . . . you're one of them." I felt my eyes fill up with tears. "It's like . . . oh, just forget it."

"No, tell me. It's like what?"

"It's like . . . the more pregnant Sarah gets, the weirder *you* get," I blurted out. There. I had finally said what had been on my mind for weeks.

"Honey, it's just that when you have a child, you want the best for them—"

"But I'm your child, too!" I replied as the tears began to fall. "And I didn't have any of those things. So what does that mean? That you didn't want the best for me?"

It's not like I wanted to be like most of my classmates and have so many extracurricular activities that my closet was overflowing with instruments and sports equipment. But the way he was talking, it was like he thought Ziggy was going to grow up to be president while I was going to work at a fast-food restaurant or something.

"And not only that, but all that stuff you're doing— with the sage, and that sloshing-water CD—"

"Lucy, Sarah thinks that—"

"That's exactly it!" I exploded. "It's like everything out of your mouth is 'Sarah this' or 'Ziggy that'! I know that you and Mom are divorced, and I'm in New York, but sometimes I feel like you've just gone ahead and made this new family and you don't care anything about your old one!"

"Lucy, nothing could be further from the truth," he said. "I'm really sorry you've been feeling this way, and I'm glad you finally told me. Because you know what Sarah says—"

I rolled my eyes. "That you live longer if you don't keep your feelings bottled up inside you."

"Exactly. And in a few weeks, when you're up here for the baby shower, we'll spend some quality time together. Just the two of us—"

"But the shower isn't until the end of October."

"Actually, we've made it a little earlier. That's part of why I called. It's now going to be the first Saturday in October."

"But that's two days before the election!" I cried. "That's totally unfair! I need to be in New York for the last-minute campaigning!"

"Sweetie, I'm sorry, but we have to move it," Dad said.

"Why?" I demanded.

"Astrid, the astrologer down at the yoga studio, told Sarah that there's a very lucky new moon that particular Saturday," Dad explained. "And if the sheep's tooth that's been blessed by the Mongolian monk that she ordered off eBay arrives in time, it will be the perfect time to do a ritual so that your baby is born with a high IQ."

Sheep's teeth? Mongolian monks? Again with the weirdness. I waited for him to say something like "Just kidding!" but he didn't. "So when you're here, we'll do something really special together. Just the two of us. Okay?"

"I think I just heard the doorbell ring," I said as I wiped my eyes. "So I have to go now."

According to the Official Parker-Moses Family Rules, hanging up the phone while mad (#33) was almost as bad as going to sleep angry (#7), but at that moment I didn't care that I was breaking any rules.

Plus, now that Dad was part of his *own* family—one that he didn't really seem to care if I joined or not—he probably didn't even notice.

Mom gives me all this grief about overlistening, but the truth is she does it herself sometimes. Which is why, that night after dinner, Alan called an Emergency Parker-Moses Family Meeting, forcing me to TiVo the special on Animal Planet called *Oh, You Animal, You!* about mating habits across the animal kingdom.

It wasn't an official family meeting, on account of the fact that part of the family (Laurel) was working. Which was a good thing, because what happened at the meeting was so embarrassing, I would have died if she had been there to see it.

"I'm not letting the campaign get in the way of my homework. I swear," I said as I sat across from them. "I mean, yes, okay, I didn't do so great on that first algebra quiz, but—"

"This isn't about your schoolwork," Mom said.

"It's not?" I asked, relieved.

"Wait, just how 'not great' are we talking about here?" Alan asked suspiciously.

"You know, I don't actually remember," I said quickly. Actually, I did. I had gotten an 80. "So what's it about then?"

Mom pulled out a Barnes & Noble bag and handed it to me. "We thought we could read these and discuss them."

"Together. As a family," Alan added.

I froze. "But I already know about the facts of life. We've been over them like ten times." I couldn't believe Mom and Alan were so desperate for stuff for us to do as a family that we had to talk about puberty.

Mom shook her head. "That's not what they are. Just open the bag."

When I did, I found two books. Both were written for kids who were preschool age. "*A Baby Sister for Onyx* and *Isn't This Fun!*" I read aloud. One had a picture of a cat and a kitten, while the other had an adult and a baby penguin.

"They're books about adjusting to a new sibling," Mom explained.

"Unfortunately, the only other books they had on the subject were really dense psychology ones," Alan explained. "So I figured while these may skew a little young, they'd still be helpful."

A *little* young? They looked like they were for three-year-olds.

"The *sentiment* is the same," agreed Mom. "So why don't we read them and then we can discuss what feelings they bring up for you."

I looked at them. "You're joking, right?"

They shook their heads.

I sighed. Did I now have to be worried that not just *one* of my parents had gone crazy but *three*? I couldn't believe they thought baby books would somehow solve my problems, because they wouldn't. The only thing that could possibly do that was if I could somehow push the Rewind button on my life and go back to when things were semi-normal. Like when my frister was still talking to me and my father wasn't obsessed with a kid who wasn't even here yet.

I picked up the book with the cats and flipped the pages. That being said, the illustrations *were* pretty cool.

And at least it would take my mind off the election for a few minutes.

But two days later, as I stood in front of 157 seventh graders, a bunch of teachers, and a few janitors, I was back to worrying about the election. Through Miss Piggy, Laurel had given me some suggestions about how not to be nervous when standing in front of a bunch of people. Like picturing them in their underwear, or pretending they were foreigners who didn't speak English, so it didn't matter what I said because they wouldn't understand me anyway.

But that morning none of the suggestions worked. In fact, the pretending-they're-foreigners one actually hurt me, because it caused me to talk really, really loud, which, when you're talking into a microphone, is not a good idea. Especially when the microphone starts doing that annoying feedback thing with screeching.

"Whoops. Sorry about that," I said loudly into it, cringing when it did it again while the crowd covered their ears. I squinted at the piece of notebook paper that Alice was holding up in front of her in the front row. Because it was written in pink ink, it was really hard to read.

"What does that say?" I whispered.

"It says 'Ex-nay on the foreigner stuff . . . go back to pretending everyone's naked or in kindergarten,'" she yelled.

I turned bright red. "Umm ... so where was I," I mumbled.

"You were at the 'And if I'm elected president, there are many things I plan to do in order to bridge the gap between the Haves and the Have-Nots and to get rid of the horrible problem of Mean People–ism in this school," Beatrice called out. Because of the control-freak thing, Beatrice had ended up memorizing my speech as well.

"Oh right. And if I'm elected president, there are many things I plan to do in order to bridge the gap between the Haves and the Have-Nots and to get rid of the horrible problem of Mean People–ism in this school," I yelled into the microphone.

As to what those things were, I wasn't quite sure yet on account of the fact I had been spending most of my time coming up with campaign slogans such as GOT BRAINS? VOTE FOR LUCY B. PARKER. I had been hoping that this would be when people would start getting really inspired—maybe a wave of excited whispers that grew into a cheer. Instead, all I got was a bunch of yawns, because it was about a billion degrees in the auditorium. And Philip Dirkin picking his nose.

Just then, Nicole Pennaker's hand shot up and started waving around.

I turned to Dr. Rem-Wall, who was seated on the corner of the stage. She was blinking a lot, the way I did when it was late and I was trying to stay awake to watch the end of a movie. "Wait a minute—there was nothing in the election rules about having to answer *questions* during this speech," I said. Especially questions from Nicole, a girl who could recite the entire school handbook and then followed every rule to a T. I couldn't call on her! But if I didn't answer questions, then it would look like I was unprepared and hadn't totally thought out my campaign. Which … was kind of true.

"Yes, Nicole?" I asked nervously. I was so getting my period right then—I just knew it.

"And what exactly is it that you intend to do?" she demanded.

"Do when?"

She rolled her eyes. "If you're elected president," she said.

"I already told you—I'm going to work to make it so that there are no more Have-Nots. Everyone will be a Have," I said proudly.

"Yeah, but how exactly are you going to do that?"

This was getting worse by the second. Why did people have to be so into *details*? Laurel was like that, too. "Unfortunately, I can't really tell you right now on account of the fact that a lot of those ways are big surprises," I replied. "You know, because of how good they are." Great. Now instead of spending my Saturday at the movies seeing Connor and Austin's new movie *Baboon Bros*, I'd be cooped up in the apartment trying to come up with these great surprises.

"Give us a hint!" Sam Meltzer called out.

I looked over to Team Have-Not for help, but they looked just as panicked as I felt. "We're, uh, still working on fine-tuning them, but when we have, I'll be sure to post them on LucyB4Prez.com." A website that we hadn't gotten up yet because we hadn't been able to decide on a background color. (I, of course, wanted purple, but Beatrice said some of the boy voters might find it a little girly.) "So be sure to check back there regularly for updates." I started to make my way off the stage and then turned and went back to the microphone. "Thank you very much for your time," I added as more feedback screeched through the room. "And in case you forgot, my name is Lucy B. Parker. But if you *do* forget, that's okay, too, since, because I'm the only other person running against Cristina Pollock, it won't be hard to find my name on the ballot." More feedback. "Well, uh, see ya," I blurted before I ran off for good this time

Finally, I was finished. I'd made it through the entire speech, plus an unexpected question! Other than the microphone issue, the sweat stains, and the idea that I wasn't able to answer the question about what things I intended to do if elected president, I thought the whole thing had gone great.

At least until Cristina walked on stage and a huge

burst of applause began. As I looked around, I realized it wasn't just the popular kids who were clapping for her, or the semi-popular ones, or even the just-normal ones. It was the seriously *un*popular kids, too. The same ones who had come up to me when no one was around to tell me how glad they were that I was running because Cristina needed to be stopped. Okay, that was so not fair. Talk about two-faced. If I hadn't been so desperate, I would have made an announcement telling them I had no interest in their votes.

But as I watched them suck up to her—clapping even louder than the popular people—I realized that they just wanted Cristina to stop being mean to them. Which I totally understood because I wanted Cristina to stop being mean to *me*, too. But still, it wasn't like I was going to *clap* for her. Until I realized that not clapping probably looked very rude and unpresidential-like, which is why I did clap. But just a little.

"Hi, everyone. Thanks sooooo much for coming today," Cristina said with a big smile after all the applause stopped. "I'd tell you my name," she continued, "but I think everyone here already knows it, seeing that I've been at the top of every 'Most Popular' list—official and unofficial—since second grade."

More clapping. This was not good. In fact, seeing the crowd acting like Hannah Montana was standing in front of them and she had barely said anything yet was pretty bad. And what drove me the most nuts about this whole thing was that when other people were looking (i.e., teachers), Cristina acted like she was a Nice Person, and because she was so believable, you'd never have known that, really, she was a Mean Person.

"I'm going to keep this short, as I'm sure everyone wants to get to lunch. Oh, and by the way? If I'm elected president, I'm going to try my best to get them to put in an all-you-can-eat sushi bar in the cafeteria." She looked over at me "*Some* of us are actually prepared for this thing."

"Wait a minute—she can't do that!" Beatrice cried over the roar of applause and whoo-hooing. "She's never going to be able to pull that off. That's false advertising! I'm going to look into suing her. That would totally get her disqualified."

Not to mention that *some* people—i.e., ME—hated seafood of any kind other than fried clam rolls from Friendly's.

"All I wanted to say is that I'd be more than happy to tell you guys what I plan to do when I'm president because it's all really awesome stuff. Like, in addition to the sushi bar, I'm going to try and get us half-day Fridays."

With that one, I had to cover my ears because the whooping was so loud.

"Plus, I'm working on an essay about how a class trip to the Bahamas in January would help us get better grades because not only would we be tan, but we'd be all relaxed and therefore in good moods."

The whooping got louder. This time even Mr. Eagle Eye got into it. Well, at least until Dr. Remington-Wallace shot him a dirty look.

Nicole Pennaker waved her hand around wildly. Finally. Someone to put Cristina in her place.

"Yes, Nicole?" Cristina asked, all fakey sweet. The reason I knew she was being fake is because once when I was in the girls' bathroom checking to see if I had gotten my period, I overheard Cristina telling Chloe how annoying Nicole was because she took her hall monitor position way too seriously.

"What I want to know—" Nicole began.

"By the way, I *love* your cardigan," Cristina gushed.

Another lie! Just minutes before the assembly I was overlistening and heard her say to Marni that she thought that it made Nicole look like a pumpkin.

"Really? You do?" Nicole asked, blushing so that she really did look like a pumpkin. "Thanks. When I saw it, it reminded me of that really pretty blue one you have."

What was wrong with these people?! Was everyone totally desperate to be popular? I could see Cristina's act working on some of the not-so-smart kids, but Nicole got the best grades in class after Francesca Leoni. You'd think she could see through this stuff.

"I'm sorry, I interrupted you," Cristina said sweetly. "That was very rude of me. Now what was your question?"

Oh please. She was being so fakey sweet it was giving me a cavity. "Oh, that's okay," Nicole said, just as butt-kissy. "I think it's awesome that you've put so much thought into all of this. The half days, and the sushi bar, and the class trip to the Bahamas all sound really great. But I was wondering . . . even though some of your other opponents don't appear to have a clear idea of what they'd do—"

I slunk down in my chair. Seeing that I was the *only* other opponent, that would be me she was talking about.

"—she *did* bring up an important issue. Which is the fact that there's a big gap here at the Center between the popular and unpopular," she continued. "Can you maybe give us a hint of what you plan to do about that?"

"That's a *fantastic* question, Nicole!" Cristina exclaimed.

Her smile was so big I'm surprised she didn't blind people with the glint off her braces. "It is? Really? I'm so glad!"

I didn't even try to stop my eyes from rolling.

Cristina looked over at Team Have, aka Tweedle Dee and Tweedle Dumber, aka Chloe and Marni. "Guys, what was it again that I was thinking about when it came to the Have/Have-Not thing?"

The two of them looked blank.

"*Remember*, Marni?" she demanded. "That thing you brought up right before assembly?"

From the look on Marni's face, she didn't. "Uhhh . . ."

"That *really, really* good idea I had?"

"Oh . . . you mean. . . . the thing that's kind of like the Big Sister/Big Brother program, except it's like Popular/Not-Popular?" Marni asked.

Wait a minute—that *was* a good idea.

"Yes! Exactly!" Cristina replied, relieved. "So can you explain the idea to Nicole, please? You know how you're so much better at doing that than I am." She flashed a smile.

Marni looked nervous. "Okay, um, so you know how they have Take-Your-Daughter-to-Work Day?"

Nicole nodded.

"Well, what we'd have is something called . . . Hang-Out-with-Your-Unpopular-Friend Day," she explained. "And what would happen is, a popular person would adopt an unpopular one for the day."

"And the unpopular one would get to sit with them at lunch, and become their friend on Facebook," Cristina interrupted. "And if there was a sleepover going on that weekend, they could come to the sleepover. That kind of stuff."

A bunch of whispered "Wow—that's an awesome idea"s and "She's really put a lot of thought into this thing"s spread through the auditorium. I tried to keep my sigh as quiet and non-frustrated-sounding as possible, but it was hard. Here she was, getting credit for something that wasn't even *her* idea—it was Marni's.

As the crowd began to clap loudly, I slunk down in my chair and gave a louder sigh. It wasn't like they could hear me over the applause.

If this was how the election was going to go, I was in big trouble.

chapter 6

Dear Dr. Maude,

Okay, so here's a question for you. Why is it that SOME people—i.e., Cristina Pollock—have lives where everything seems to go right for them? Like they have really long shiny hair? And their forehead barely ever breaks out? And they're constantly number one in the Who Will Win the Seventh-Grade Class President Race? poll that Dinshaw Saigal set up on his blog and updates every hour because he's really good with computers and has figured out a way to do that?

And then there are OTHER people—i.e., me—who have lives where it's not just enough that they have to deal with ONE horrible thing (like constantly being number two on Dinshaw's poll, which translates to last, since there are only two people running) but a BUNCH of horrible things. Like, say, a frister who talks to her only through her cat. And a father who is obsessed with babies who aren't even here yet. And boobs that just keep growing. (The other night at dinner, Mom put down her fork and, in front of Alan, said, "Lucy, I can't believe I'm saying this, but it looks like you've outgrown your new bra that we just got you a month ago!")

Anyway, the reason I'm writing is because I have a favor to ask. Even though we've never met, I hope that you know me well enough to believe that I'd make an awesome class president. And because we've now gotten to the video portion of Operation Election, I thought maybe one day after school, we could come down to your apartment with a video camera and tape a little interview between you and me.

Like we could talk about the problem of Mean People–ism, and I could tell you how I plan to stop it and you could say stuff like "Lucy, those are all fantastic ideas, and if I were a seventh grader at the Center for Creative Learning, you'd definitely have MY vote!" (BTW, you don't have to worry about memorizing any of that. We have a ton of poster board, so Malia's going to write it all down in really big letters on cue cards for you because she's got the best handwriting of all of us. Well, Laurel's is even better than Malia's, but because we're not talking because she hates me, I can't really ask her.)

If you'd be willing to do this, I'd be so so so SO grateful! Obviously, I can't pay you for your time because Alan, who's a lawyer, says it's illegal to pay people to have them say that they'd vote for you. But I'd be happy to give you some extra buttons. For free. And obviously, if

I am elected, I will make sure to give you a huge shout-out in my acceptance speech.

Let me know.

yours truly,
Lucy B. Parker

Luckily, after the speech, things started to turn around. Not everything—not with Laurel, or with Dad—but with the campaign. Spending lunch periods walking around to the different tables in the cafeteria so I could introduce myself to the kids I didn't know well (which, for someone who sat in Alaska, was about 90 percent of them), I discovered that the two things they wanted more than anything were longer summer vacations and no report cards. Those seemed like real long shots, but I promised them I'd do my best. And with the *Everything You Ever Wanted to Know About Lucy B. Parker ... But Were Afraid to Ask* page on LucyB4Prez.com (we had finally decided on a multicolored polka-dot background), they were getting to know *me*. Like, say, the fact that I loved color. And could touch my nose with my tongue. (For some reason that one was really impressive to people.)

But I think it was Malia's brilliant idea that really turned things around. After snapping a bunch of photos of kids around the school, she put together a collage. On one side of the poster board were the "Haves"—they were the ones sitting at the more popular tables toward the middle of the cafeteria, laughing and having a good time, with cool clothes and minimal zittage. And on the other side were the "Have-Nots"—and they were looking a little sad and a bit lonely, like the pets waiting to be adopted at Petco. At the bottom of the poster in bubble letters done by Alice (not as bubbly as Laurel's but bubbly enough) it said "Lucy B. Parker: Committed to Turning the Have-Nots into Haves!"

Beatrice's suggestion to put it up right outside the cafeteria so that everyone would see it was genius. Suddenly, I started getting notes from kids—both signed and anonymous—about how grateful they were that someone finally had the guts to acknowledge in public how totally unfair it was that the popular kids were the ones who got to be popular. Now that the speeches were over and kids didn't have to worry about acting cool in front of Cristina, they weren't as scared to start backing me. According to Dinshaw, my numbers were rising every day. Cristina was still in the lead—especially after announcing on her website that any girl who voted for her and could prove it would get to sit next to her for twenty minutes at lunch—but suddenly the idea that maybe I had a shot at winning went from "absolutely positively no way" to "probably no way." Which, as far as I was concerned, was a huge improvement.

But Alice's videotaping skills? Not so much improvement there.

"Alice, how did you manage to push the Mute button?" I sighed as Team Have-Not watched the video she had just shot of Pete in the lobby of the Conran. This time we were using my camera. According to Pete, his Puerto Rican heritage makes him emotional and passionate. Which is why when he talked about what a great person I was and how in less than a year I had already become one of the best-liked people in the building because I always made sure to hold the elevator for people, it was very moving.

Well, at least it was the first time. Alice somehow erased the first take, and then somehow managed to put her hand in front of the lens the second time. So by the third time he sounded like a very fake radio announcer. Not that it mattered, because of the Mute button thing.

"Since this video thing doesn't look like it's gonna work, if you want, I could come to your school on my day off," Pete offered. "You know, do a Q&A about you. Like whatchamacallit—Show and Tell, but with a real live person."

"Thanks, Pete," I replied. "But I think a video would be better." As much as I loved him, once he started talking it was hard to shut him up.

"Let me just try one more time," Alice said, grabbing for the camera.

"No. It's okay," I said, trying to hold on to it.

"I'll be more careful this time," she said, trying to yank it away from me.

As I yanked back, it went flying through the air and landed with a big thud. Followed by a cracking noise.

"Whoops," she said.

I picked it up to find the lens full of spiderweb-looking cracks, and sighed. "I think the whole video thing might be a waste of time anyway," I said. "Maybe we can just keep focusing on posters."

Beatrice looked up from her laptop. "Uh-oh," she said.

"What?" I asked, panicked. I knew Beatrice well enough to know the difference in her *Uh-oh*'s, and this was definitely on the this-is-not-good end of the scale.

"Dinshaw just updated his site. Your numbers are down a ton."

"What? Why?" I cried as I ran over to see for myself. She was right. That morning I had been at 32 percent, but now I was down to 20 percent. "Scroll down to the Day in Review part," I said. Dinshaw had recently added a section to the site where he recapped the election news of the day with stuff like "Today, Lucy B. Parker distributed Hershey Kisses to the voters, which didn't go over as well as M&M's and Skittles that Cristina handed out. But the word jumble Lucy distributed after lunch was pretty cool and gave students something to do for the rest of the afternoon. Which, because it was Pizza Tuesday, was helpful because everyone knows that that post-pizza coma makes it hard to concentrate in class."

"Rumor has it that one of the candidates is going to set up a Make-Your-Own-Sundae bar in the next few days," Beatrice read out loud. "Hint: it's not the candidate with a middle initial of B."

"Ooh really?" Alice gasped. "Does it say when?"

Beatrice gave her a look. "Not only that," she continued reading, "but my sources tell me that there may be some swag bags floating around the school soon."

"Swag bags?" I cried. "That's so not fair!" We didn't have them back in Northampton, but swag bags were very big in New York. Basically they were super-fancy loot bags, but instead of candy and fake tattoos, they were filled with stuff like watches and makeup and gift certificates for free facials and massages. Laurel always got them at the events she went to. And then, lots of times, she would give them to me. But that was back when we were friends, so I doubted I'd be getting them anymore.

"Does it say how someone goes about getting one?" Alice asked.

"Alice, do you not realize we're talking about the enemy here?" Beatrice asked.

She shrugged. "I know, but I bet they're really awesome because of her mom." Voted "Number One Party Planner" by *New York* magazine that year, Cristina's mom had tons of connections.

"Okay, this is not good," Beatrice said. "Not only do we need a video, but it's got to be awesome." She sighed.

"I really hate that I have to do this, but I think the time has come."

"To do what?" I asked.

"To force my brother to make the video for us. He *was* president of the AV club at his school last year, so you can't get better than that."

I felt my hands get all clammy. I had seen Beatrice's brother Blair only a few times in passing since he came back from camp, so I still wasn't sure whether I wanted him to be my local crush. I guess some people would say that having to spend time together on a video would be the perfect opportunity to find out, but I knew myself, and I knew it would make me even more nervous. "Um, I don't know about that," I said anxiously.

Beatrice looked me. "Look, Lucy, buttons and Hershey Kisses and word jumbles may cut it in Northampton elections, but this is Manhattan," she said. "We have to pull out the big guns. Even if they are completely obnoxious and annoying."

"Or we could just go back to my idea about offering voters a walk-on on Laurel's show," Alice said.

"Okay. Fine. He can do the video." Anything was better than asking Laurel for help. Even though, by this point, she probably wouldn't help me anyway. "But let me be the one to ask him. I don't want him to think I'm one of those candidates who just makes people run around doing things for her all the time," I blurted.

Oh no, what had I just done? Now I had to actually *talk* to Blair?

"Okay," Beatrice shrugged. "But you need to do it soon. We only have a week of campaigning left."

Maybe Malia was right. Maybe there *was* a bright side to all this drama. Because if anything would bring on my period, having to be around Blair Lerner-Moskovitz for huge chunks of time would probably do it.

After dinner, when Beatrice texted me that Blair had just gotten home from his guitar lesson, I went down to their apartment on the tenth floor to ask him. Well, I went down after changing out of my powder-blue Hello Kitty T-shirt and into my purple butterfly one because it made my boobs look smaller. And after applying a bunch of Dr Pepper Lip Smacker before wiping it off and putting on some Starburst Mango Melon instead. And after practicing what I was going to say five times in front of my mirror.

And getting busted by Laurel in the process.

"Miss Piggy, can you please tell Lucy that she might want to lose the part where she tells Blair she can't find anyone else in Manhattan who knows how to use a video camera, which is the only reason she's asking him," I heard her say through my door to the cat, who was trying to reach her tail but, because she was so fat, kept rolling over on her side. "If that was in a script that was given to me, I'd definitely have a talk with the director about it. I mean, it doesn't really ring true."

I turned bright red. Obviously, I hadn't closed my door all the way. I turned around and glared at her. "Miss Piggy, can you please tell Laurel that she might want to stop SPYING on people? And that while she may get to boss around the writers on her show, this particular scene has nothing to do with her." That being said, maybe the idea that I couldn't find anyone else who knew how to work a video camera was pushing it. Laurel's face got all crinkly, like the time when she read that article in one of the gossip magazines that said she was an alien who had been sent here to spy on humans. "I don't boss anyone around!" she cried.

I snorted. "Oh yeah? Then what do you call what you were doing with my campaign?" I demanded. "Before I had even decided I wanted to *run*."

"I told you! I was just trying to *help*."

"There's a difference between helping, and giving a person a five-page to-do list," I replied. "*That* is bossing around!"

"I didn't realize it was such a crime to be a little organized!" she snapped.

I snorted again. "A *little* organized?"

She waved her hand around my room. "Oh. Excuse me. I forgot who I was talking to. Obviously they don't believe in organization back in Massachusetts."

Wait a minute. It was one thing to get on me about

the fact that I tended to keep things a teensy bit—okay, fine, a lot—on the messy side. It was another to bring an entire state into it. That was totally unfair. "Yeah, well, sometimes I wish I was still there!" I yelled. I didn't really. What I wished for was that things were like they had been before Laurel and I had started fighting, when she actually liked having me around.

"If that's how you feel, maybe you should go back there!" she yelled back.

So I was right! Laurel *didn't* want me here. All that my-house-is-your-house stuff she had always been talking about? Just one big giant lie. It only sounded true because she was an actress and was paid a lot of money to be able to make people believe things that weren't true.

"Yeah, well, maybe I will!" I shouted before slamming the door in her face.

Except even if I wanted to go back to Northampton (and I didn't), I couldn't. Not unless I wanted to sleep on a sofa bed and be ignored.

When I got down to the Lerner-Moskovitz's door, my arm somehow became paralyzed, making it impossible to raise it and knock. I was, however, able to walk into the stairwell to practice my little speech again.

"You can do this," I said aloud when I was done. "He's just a *boy*. And not even a particularly cute one at that. In fact, most girls might think—"

"Um, what are you *doing*?" a voice asked a second later.

I turned around to see Blair standing there holding a bag of garbage. His brown hair was all hat-head-y, his glasses were crooked, and he had a few stains on his Star Wars T-shirt. But other than that he looked good.

"What did you hear?" I demanded.

"Nothing. But what are you doing?"

"Nothing," I said, as if it was perfectly normal for me to be sitting in the stairwell near the garbage chute. "I was just . . . hanging out . . . meditating." *Please don't start bloversharing,* I thought. "My parents are Buddhists, so they do that a lot," I babbled. This was so unfair. It was like instead of restless leg syndrome, which was this disease that Beatrice had been sure she had last week after reading about it on the Internet, I had restless lips syndrome. "Actually, my dad a lot more than my mom," I went on. "'Cause she's got adult-onset ADHD. And Sarah—that's my dad's girlfriend—she meditates a lot, too. Even though she's pregnant and ginormous because she's eating so much that it's hard for her to sit cross-legged on the floor nowadays."

Blair was looking at me like I was crazy. Maybe because *I WAS.* Why oh why couldn't I stop talking?

"Anyway, I find stairwells a really good place to meditate," I continued. "Because they're so . . . relaxing." I hauled myself to my feet. "But funny I should run into you because I was actually coming to see you."

"You were? Why?" he asked, all suspicious.

"Because I'm running for class president," I replied. "And according to your sister, if there's any chance of me winning, I have to have a really awesome video." I held up the camera. "Except now my camera is broken. And no one I know really knows how to use it anyway."

"Let me see it."

I handed it to him. He went to turn it on, but all that happened was the motor made this really sad *whomp-whomp-whomp* noise. "Wow. You really managed to screw this up," he said.

I sighed. "Tell me about it."

"So if I did it . . . what's in it for me?"

I thought about it. "You like cupcakes?"

He wrinkled his nose. "Cupcakes? Do I *look* like a girl?"

Obviously he didn't. But with his belly that looked to be on the squishy side, he also didn't look like the kind of person who ever said no to dessert. "Okay. Fine. Name your favorite dessert, then."

"Fried Oreos," he said smugly.

Wow. I loved those, too. That being said, it wasn't a fair answer. Everyone knew those were almost as difficult to track down as Coca-Cola cake. With the Oreos, it was basically street fairs or bust. "Fine. I'll get you some of those.

"*Fine.* I'll do it."

"You will?"

He nodded.

"Omigod—that's awesome!"

"It's not about being nice," he grumbled. "It's about fried Oreos. And the fact that I get a stomachache when I think about the idea of completely unqualified people abusing innocent electronic equipment." He started to walk back toward the hall. "We can start tomorrow," he said. "I've got guitar at ten, Upper West Side Chess Club at noon, PSAT prep at two, and the Gamers of the Upper West Side Awards at eight, but I could fit you in at four."

Jeez—all that on a *Saturday*? The only plans I had were to figure out a way to avoid cleaning my room. "Okay," I said. "I think I can fit that in."

He nodded. "Okay. See you," he said.

"See you," I mumbled as he walked into the hall.

I plopped back down onto the steps. Oh my God. My maybe-local-crush had just offered to help me with my campaign. Which meant I'd get to know him better.

I couldn't decide if this was the best news ever . . . or the worst. Sure, the whole bloversharing thing hadn't ended up totally out of control, and I had been able to talk to him normally after a while, but that was for only, about, like two minutes. Having to do a video together meant MANY minutes together. Many minutes where I would have the chance to embarrass myself. While there was nothing in the crush log rules about your crush having to like you back, I don't think that having him hate you would be considered helpful.

But even worse than that was, what if, in hanging out with him and getting to know him, I decided that I didn't like *him*? Then I'd be back to square one with this whole crush thing and I'd have to find someone else.

Which sounded about as fun as talking to Sarah's belly.

Unlike some people who love when there's a video camera being aimed at them—like, say, Marissa and Alice, who completely hog the camera—I'm not a fan. What usually happens is my mouth gets all dry, and when I talk, it sounds like I have marbles rolling around in it. And if the person behind the camera happens to be not just a boy, but a boy who, as you hang out with him more, you realize you *don't* hate because he's not super-awful but instead is indeed a serious contender for your local crush, then the marbles are more like giant boulders which makes it so you can't open your mouth at all.

"And cutting!" Blair yelled the next afternoon in Strawberry Fields, the part of Central Park that was named in honor of John Lennon because he used to live in an apartment building called the Dakota right near it. For the fourth time, after getting out, "Hi. My name is Lucy B. Parker, and here's why I think you should vote for me for seventh-grade class president," I had completely clammed up and forgotten how to talk.

"Sorry," I said, wiping the sweat off my forehead. Beatrice flopped back on the grass with a giant sigh.

"Look, I don't want to tell you how to do your job or anything," Blair said as a glop of fried Oreo fell on his Atari T-shirt. (After hitting three street fairs that morning, I had finally found some at the Western Manhattan Chamber of Commerce one, at Amsterdam and Eightieth.) "But when people vote for a president, they usually want someone who knows how to take charge. And *talk*."

"She *is* take charge. And she *can* talk," Beatrice snapped. "She just has a little bit of stage fright. Why do you have to be such a jerk all the time?" She turned to me. "I can't believe you asked him to do this." Beatrice thought that her brother was the second most annoying person on the planet. Right after Asher Kulik, a kid in our grade who smelled like mothballs and was constantly getting his tongue caught in binder clips.

"Huh? You *made* me ask him!" I reminded her.

"That's because I was on cold medicine. You shouldn't listen to me on cold medicine. My nose was all stuffed up."

"How could your nose possibly be stuffed up?" Blair asked. "It's so big you could fit a bus in there."

Beatrice stood up. "My nose is not big!" she cried.

Now it was my turn to flop down on the grass and sigh. Beatrice was very sensitive when it came to her nose. It *was* kind of big.

Blair snorted. "Yeah, right. You better hope that your bat mitzvah present is a nose job."

I wondered if this was how it was going to be between Ziggy and me. Probably not. With all of the crazy things my dad and Sarah were doing, he'd be so perfect he'd never say anything mean.

Beatrice turned to me. "Sorry, Lucy—I know I'm your campaign manager, but that doesn't mean I have to sit here and listen to someone so bourgeois." Although we had been BFFs for a while, I still wasn't exactly sure what *bourgeois* meant. I knew it was French, and I knew it was some sort of insult in the annoying/stupid family, but whenever I pressed Beatrice to tell me what it meant, she never gave me a straight answer. She started stomping toward the exit to the park. "You're on your own with this!" she announced over her shoulder.

"But this video was your idea!" I shouted after her, even though she'd already stomped away and couldn't hear me. I rolled over. "Who am I kidding? I'm awful in front of the camera."

Blair twisted his top lip and pulled it up so it touched his nose. I had learned this afternoon that he did that when he was thinking really hard. It was incredibly weird-looking, but from the number of times he did it, it was obvious that he was a very deep thinker. According to my dad, that was a very good quality for a person to have. In fact, I bet at that very moment he was looking online for a book called *How to Train Your Baby to Be an Incredibly Deep Thinker.*

Blair let go of his lip. "I have an idea," he announced. "Not only that, but it's one of my brilliant ones."

Uh-oh. The first brilliant idea Blair had come up with that morning had to do with my jumping out of a plane and when the parachute unfurled, it would say, WANT A PRESIDENT WHO'S FEARLESS? LOOK NO FURTHER THAN LUCY B. PARKER! Luckily, Beatrice had immediately nixed that by saying we barely had enough campaign funds for glitter pens, let alone a plane. "What is it?" I asked warily.

"I think that instead of you trying to be all I'm-Lucy-B.-Parker-and-I'm-running-for-president, you should just, I don't know . . . be yourself," he said.

I rolled my eyes. *More* of this being-myself stuff? Pete was always going on about that. Did these people not realize that myself was sort of goofy, with not much coordination, and the bad habits of bloversharing AND overlistening? Those weren't qualities you wanted in a president. I wanted to be. . . . presidential-like. Like Cristina Pollock, minus the meanness.

"What do you mean 'myself'?"

He shrugged. "Like how you are when you and my sister are hanging out in her room," he said. "You know . . . funny. Like you are when you imitate that Dr. Maude lady."

If I was lucky, maybe there'd be an earthquake at that moment and the ground would crack open and swallow me up. "You *saw* that?" I squeaked. "Were you *spying* on us?"

"*No,*" he said defensively. Was it my imagination or was he turning red? "I just happened to be walking by Beatrice's room at the exact moment you were pacing around the room with your hand on your hips yelling, 'What part of "Get with the program" do you people not understand?' in a New York accent, like she does on TV, and I had to lean down and tie my shoelace or risk tripping on it and breaking my neck and ending up paralyzed and in a wheelchair for life."

I couldn't believe Blair had seen me being so . . . *me.* Or, in that particular moment, Dr. Maude. I didn't even want to imagine what other embarrassing things he may have seen. It was better if I didn't know. "What else did you see?" I demanded.

He shrugged. "Nothing, really."

I exhaled the gallon of air that I had been holding in my lungs. Phew.

"I mean, other than when you were pretending to be a character in one of those Spanish soap opera things. You know, talking in a bad Spanish accent and yelling *Ay, caramba* as you kept flinging yourself down on the bed."

He had seen me pretending to be Guadalupe from *Amantes*, the telenovela that Rose and I watched? Could there *be* anything more embarrassing than that?

"Oh, and that time you were pretending to be a contestant on *American Idol* even though your voice isn't all that good."

Apparently, yes—yes, there was something more embarrassing. I couldn't believe that after seeing all that, Blair would even talk to me, let alone agree to help me make this video. "So let me get this straight—you want me to act like a total dork in front of the camera?" I asked. "*That'll* win me a lot of votes."

"No. Not that stuff. *Especially* not the singing part, please," he said. "But we'll just pretend that . . . I don't know . . . I'm Beatrice. Even though, if you ask me, that would be the worst curse in the world. And we're sitting in her room instead of here in Central Park in front of a bunch of tourists," he went on. "I'll just ask you questions, and you'll answer them."

I gave him a doubtful look.

"Come on, it'll be easy."

I looked around. At least they were friendly looking tourists. My eyes narrowed. "What kind of questions?" If he asked me what my bra size was, I'd kill him.

"I don't know! The kind of questions you'd ask someone who was running for class president! Just answer them, okay?"

I could tell he was starting to get annoyed. "Okay, okay."

He picked up the camera, and my stomach started to get wonky. Remembering one of the tricks that Laurel once told me she used when she got really nervous when shooting, I squinted my eyes so he got blurry, which made it easier to pretend he was Beatrice. Even though he wasn't wearing all black, it wasn't as hard I as thought, especially because his nose was kind of on the big side as well. And because I didn't get nervous when talking to Beatrice, not only did the boulders in my mouth dissolve once I started talking, but I wouldn't shut up. And not in an uh-oh, I'm-so-bloversharing kind of way.

Not only did I talk about all the stuff I planned to do if I were elected (starting with Bring-Your-Pet-to-School Day and getting softer toilet paper in the bathrooms), but I also shared my views on everything from the stuff that really bothered me about the subway (when someone spread his legs out wide so he took up two or three seats) to tips on how to get yourself out of a bad mood. ("Wear a lot of color. Or eat a few cupcakes. If you can do both, even better.")

As I did my impersonation of Alan running one of our official Parker-Moses Family Meetings ("Item number twelve: It has been brought to my attention by Rose that there was an ant spotting in the living room at approximately three forty-five p.m. on Tuesday. In light of this, all food must now be consumed in the kitchen."), Blair cracked up so hard that he had to put the camera down. Which was a good thing because I realized that that would not be good to show my entire class, even if it was accurate.

Once he managed to stop laughing, he looked at me. "You know, Lucy, you're not just funny. You're *really* funny," he said, sounding surprised.

I felt myself turn red. "I am?"

He nodded. "Yeah. Usually I can't stand Beatrice's friends, but you're, I don't know, *different . . .*"

"Different, how?" I asked nervously.

"I don't know," he said, annoyed. "Just different, okay? Like not so completely annoying you want to smother the person with a pillow."

Was that a compliment? I couldn't tell.

He stood up. "I have to get home and feed my turtle before the awards ceremony. I'll see you later."

"Okay," I said, starting to get up. "I'll walk with you."

But before I managed to get to my feet, he was already on his way. For a tubby guy, he could move *really* fast.

What's going on here? I thought as I plopped back down into the middle of Strawberry Fields. I didn't have a ton of experience with boys. Actually, other than Connor (and he wasn't really a boy-boy on account of the whole he-was-a-celebrity-who-lived-in-California thing), I had none.

With Connor, it was different. He *wanted* to hang out with me. Like walk-on-the- beach-with-me-in-Malibu hang out. And he gave me lots of compliments, like, how it was cool that I ate bread because no one else in L.A. did. But Blair didn't do any of those things. He acted annoyed and couldn't seem to get away from me fast enough. Okay, yes, one of the articles I had read online when I was researching crush symptoms had said that boys tended to act like that when *they* had crushes, but I didn't think that was the case here. I mean, the chance that the boy I had a crush on was crushing back on me? That was about as likely to happen as Laurel's sending me a text that moment saying how sorry she was that she had been such a jerk and was there any way I could possibly forgive her. Which, as I fished my phone out of my tote bag to check, had not happened.

I'd be lying if I said that hanging out with Blair that afternoon hadn't made me realize that I could do a lot worse in the crush department. But I still wasn't ready to admit it to Beatrice or put it in the log. Maybe I'd get up the guts to do that in … a year or something, but between the election, and fighting with Laurel, and being ignored by my father, I had enough on my plate. In fact, it felt like I had almost too much on my plate.

Which, for a girl who never had to be told to finish her food because there were kids starving all over the globe, was saying a lot.

chapter 7

Dear Dr. Maude,

Okay, this is not an e-mail about the campaign. Or Laurel. The reason I'm writing you today has to do with BLM. (In case you forgot, that's the abbreviation I use for Blair Lerner-Moskovitz when I don't want anyone to know that that's what I'm writing about. Like, say, now.)

It's kind of a long story so I won't go into it now, but because of this video, we ended up spending the weekend together, and Blair was acting REALLY weird around me. Like he'd say something that's along the lines of what you'd say to a crush—for instance, "You're really funny"—but then he'd get all defensive when I said something like "Really?"

A while ago I read that that kind of thing is typical behavior for boys when they have crushes, but in this case I find it hard to believe that the boy I might like might like me back. But the thing is, yesterday when I told Pete the whole story, he said that, yes, this is indeed the way that boys act when they like a girl on account of the fact that we live in a society where they're given the message that it's not okay for them to show their feelings. Except for him, because he's Latin and therefore very emotional.

Is that true, Dr. Maude? Not the Latin part, but the boy part and the way they act when they like a girl? I figured that because it has to do with feelings, you'd know the answer.

yours truly,
Lucy B. Parker

P.S. BTW—I just want to put it out there that if you ever returned my e-mails, I wouldn't have to ask Pete about this stuff. I mean, sure, he's one of my BFFs, but still he's a BOY so talking about boy stuff with him sometimes gets a little embarrassing.

As much as Beatrice couldn't stand her brother, even she had to agree that the video was the thing that really pushed me up the ranks in the poll. I couldn't believe how great it turned out. Well, except for the fact that there was a smudge of chocolate from a fried Oreo on my chin that no one bothered to tell me about.

Blair put it together the following weekend in between his guitar lesson, his PSAT class, and a signing at a bookstore by one of his favorite comic book illustrators. We ended up calling it *Just a Normal, Regular Day in the Life of Normal, Regular Lucy B. Parker,* and it was just that: me doing the normal, regular stuff I did all the time. Like hanging out in Central Park. Getting a cupcake at Billy's

Bakery. Buying a Dr Pepper at Mr. Kim's deli. We even filmed me on the M72 crosstown bus. Then, as luck would have it, just as I was talking about how I'm a big believer in karma and how important it is to be nice to everyone— even people who aren't nice to me—an old woman got on, and I got up to give her my seat, which is an excellent example of how to get good karma. I would've done it anyway, even if there weren't a camera on me, but it was cool that the timing worked out that way.

Throughout the whole thing it was just me being me, which sounds like it would be pretty boring, but the way Blair edited it together, plus how he used Laurel's hit song "Believe in Yourself," made it really interesting. (When I asked her through Miss Piggy, she said it was okay to use the song.)

Plus, it was actually REALLY funny. I think part of the reason for that was because I'm wearing so much color (the rainbow-sequined Chuck Taylors that Laurel gave me looked really cool on camera), and I'm surrounded by people wearing mostly all black. But it also could be the fact that even though I fought him on it, Blair kept in some of the moments where I was having coordination issues. Usually I get really embarrassed when that happens in front of other people, but in this case it added up to what Mom called "comic relief."

When we pulled it up on the class computer before homeroom Monday morning, I was beyond nervous. Especially because Cristina's video—which we had just watched—had been done by an Academy Award–winning director who was friends with her parents. But after we were done playing it, everyone clapped really loud.

All day kids were coming up to me saying, "Wow, I had no idea you were so funny!" I still wasn't sure why—I was just being me—but it's not like I was going to disagree with them. Especially if it meant a vote. By Tuesday morning, it had gotten 112 hits on YouTube, which was pretty impressive. Maybe not as impressive as the 432,987 hits that Laurel got in one hour when her new video was posted, but still, for a normal, regular kid, that's not bad.

Between the video and the chocolate chip cookies we handed out on Tuesday (unlike the first batch we made, which had triple the amount of salt because Alice has trouble following directions, they were super-yummy), I moved way up in Dinshaw's poll. Now it was 57 percent versus 43 percent, which, while not exactly neck and neck, was a lot closer than head and foot. Even when Cristina announced on her website later that night that she had decided to offer free "How to Talk to Boys" lessons to anyone who promised to vote for her, my numbers stayed up.

That night, for the first time in weeks, instead of tossing and turning as I thought about how I was going to solve all the problems in my life, I conked out right away. Well, after walking past Laurel's door a bunch of times to see if she just "happened" to open it. (She didn't.)

Maybe things with my frister were still a mess, but at least things were finally looking up on the campaign front. Which is why, before I got into bed, I took out my advice notebook and wrote, "Remember that as bad at things might seem, they can always surprise you by turning around for the better."

When I walked out into the kitchen the next day to find that Rose had brought me some fried plantains (I had never had them before we moved to New York, but they had quickly become one of my favorites), it seemed my run of good luck was continuing. And the fact that Beatrice and I were forced to take the bus to school because I had us running late due to an outfit change (I thought my Angry Little Girls Team Garlic T-shirt was really funny, but when I got down to the lobby, Beatrice said that it might turn off voters who didn't like garlic) and the bus pulled right up was another good sign. But if you're running for class president and you notice that an awful lot of people are staring at you in the morning before you even make it inside your school? That's not good. And if kids start to point and whisper when you do make it inside? That's even worse. Add some giggles to that? You know there's a problem.

And if you're walking down the hall with your friends and see a group of kids gathered together *really* laughing at you? And when you make your way through, you see that what they're laughing at is a blown-up-to-poster-size photo taken the year before on a movie set in Northampton, Massachusetts, of your egg-looking-because-of-a-Straightening-Iron-Incident head? That problem is BIG. Especially if, written underneath it in huge letters, it says, IS THIS WHO YOU WANT AS CLASS PRESIDENT?

"OMIGOD—Lucy, is that picture of the almost-bald girl *you*?!" Alice yelled. The minute she said that, anyone in the hall who hadn't been gathered around the poster walked over to see what she was looking at.

"What . . . where did . . . how the heck . . . ?" I sputtered. This couldn't be happening. I had spent almost an entire year trying to erase the Hat Incident from my memory. And now not only was it back, it was poster-size!

"Like it?" I heard Cristina Pollock's snotty voice say from behind me. "I think you look soooo cute. Kind of like that creature in that old movie *E.T.*"

Everyone started to laugh. I whipped around, swiping at the tears that had immediately formed. One of the only good things about moving and being the New Girl in a new school was that I had finally been able to leave the Hat Incident behind. At least I had, until *now*. "Where did you get that?" I demanded.

She shrugged. "I have my ways," she said as she kept walking, flipping her long blonde hair over her shoulder. Although it would have given me seriously bad karma, if I had had a pair of scissors in my tote bag, I totally would've chopped off her hair right then and there. Let *her* experience what it's like to have to wear hats every day for months until a hairdresser-to-the-stars fixes it so that you look halfway normal again.

Beatrice shook her head. "This is beyond low. Even for her." As I rummaged in my bag for a tissue, she patted my arm. "I'm so sorry, Lucy," she said. "But try to look at the bright side."

I turned to her. "The *bright* side? There's a *bright* side to having the world seeing me looking like a human egg?!"

She shrugged. "Sure. It means she knows you're gaining on her. If she wasn't worried that you had a decent chance of winning, she never would've gone to all this effort," she said. "Believe me, if I know anything about Cristina after having been best friends with her, it's that she's one of the laziest people in the world. And this took *a lot* of effort."

Any other time that would've made me feel better, but right then? Not so much. But before I could run off to the bathroom to cry in peace, there was a tap on my shoulder. "Lucy? You want a piece of this?" a boy whispered.

I turned around to find Quentin Fox, one of the geekier gamers, holding out a pack of Eclipse Winterfrost gum. Even though I got a little nervous talking to him sometimes because he had a lazy eye, which meant that I was never sure where to look, he was really nice. "It's pretty strong," he said. "Sometimes if I forget to brush my teeth before I leave my apartment in the morning, it does the trick and I'm safe." He breathed into the palm of his hand and wrinkled his nose. "Well, most of the time I am."

Huh? I breathed into my own palm. My breath was fine. "Thanks, Quentin, but why would I need gum?"

"Because of what it says on the poster of you and Connor Forrester down the hall," he replied.

My eyes widened. *What* poster of Connor and me down the hall?

Monica Barron, a member of the drama club who knew every single word to every song from the musical *Annie*, joined us. "If it makes you feel any better, I think Cristina's totally wrong—it doesn't look like he's pulling away from you because your breath stinks."

I sprinted down the hall so fast you would've thought I was a person who actually liked gym. Right next to the cafeteria, there it was: that picture that some dumb paparazzo had taken of Connor Forrester and me on the red carpet at a movie premiere in L.A. back in June that had ended up on the Internet and in the gossip magazines. Okay, yes, it *did* look like he was pulling away as I leaned forward. But that was only because he was about to sneeze and was being polite so he didn't get germs all over me.

Underneath the picture, in very large bubble letters, it said, DO YOU REALLY WANT A PRESIDENT WITH BAD BREATH? IF

NOT, VOTE FOR ME, CRISTINA POLLOCK—BECAUSE I BRUSH AFTER EVERY MEAL AND SNACK! The whole thing totally wasn't fair! I brushed my teeth a lot, too. At least twice a day. *Maybe* if I was really tired I would skip the nighttime brush, but I definitely did it at least once a day.

"Like it?" smirked Cristina. She turned to the crowd. "I'd like to invite you all to see my latest video!" she announced. "We'll be screening it in the library before homeroom starts!"

I paled as I turned to Beatrice. "Latest video? How many of these things do we have to make?" Hanging out with Blair hadn't been that bad, but it's not like I wanted to do more of it. While he went to a different school, he knew enough kids at ours that he'd definitely hear about what I was now calling the Poster Incident.

Beatrice reached in her bag for the rules and regulations, which, because we had spent so much time looking at them, were now dog-eared and smudged. "It doesn't say," she replied as she scanned them. "And because it doesn't say, I guess you can make as many as you want."

We began to follow everyone into the library. Although I had zero interest in watching Cristina flip her hair around on screen, at least it would take the attention off me. Except if the video happened to be about me. Which it was.

When you're a "Person of," like I was (that's when you're somehow connected to a Famous Person, such as a Daughter of, or a Mother of, or—in my case—a Frister of), one of the side effects is that it makes *you* famous by accident, even if that's the last thing you want. And it also makes it so that anyone—including Mean People—can go on the Internet and find pictures of you, and articles that have untrue information about you.

All of that is bad enough, but when it's strung together into a three-minute video, which, if it had a title, would be called *The Uncut Blooper Version of Lucy B. Parker's Most Embarrassing Moments*, it's beyond horrible. Photos where it looked like I was picking my nose (I wasn't), spilling something on myself (I was), or preparing to throw up (I wasn't, but I sure wanted to at that moment) flashed by. As kids howled with laughter, I just stood there, unable to move.

I looked like a complete dork. The girl up on the screen wasn't someone you'd want as your president. She was someone you'd want around just so you could laugh at her behind her back. Maybe if I was really presidential, I would have stood up and given some big speech about how wrong all of this was.

But I didn't. I couldn't.

Instead, I somehow managed to unglue my feet from the floor so I could run to the girls' room and burst into tears. It wasn't a very presidential-like thing to do, but I couldn't help it. Neither was going to the school nurse and telling her that I was pretty sure I was coming down with a very contagious disease and she needed to call my mother and let me go home. Luckily (or unluckily) for me, by that time even the faculty had seen the posters, so she felt bad for me and didn't give me a hard time. Mom didn't, either, after I gulped the story out to her in between sniffles.

"I knew I never should have listened to Laurel when she brought up the running-for-president thing," I said to her in between bites of my frozen peanut butter hot chocolate at lunch later.

Usually I wasn't allowed to have dessertlike things in the middle of the day, unless it was a special occasion. But luckily, I had a mother who knew that having your life completely ruined forever was just as important as a birthday. "In fact, this is where the whole dumb thing happened! Because she had been DD'd by the hostess!"

"What's DD again?" Mom asked.

"Dork discrimination," I replied.

"Oh, right. But honey, you can't let one bad day in your campaign ruin the whole thing—"

"Mom, please don't give me the speech about the river flowing—"

"I'm not going to. What Cristina Pollock did to you was awful. Like a ten on the scale of Mean People behavior. But for you to give up now would be to go against everything you've been talking about during your campaign."

I shook my head as I scraped the last of the frozen peanut butter from the side of the bowl. "Nice try, Mom, but the kids at the Center are going to have to watch someone else be made a fool of. I'm done."

After school, Beatrice, Alice, and Malia showed up to try to convince me I wasn't, in fact, done.

"Look, I really appreciate all the work you guys have put into this," I said from my bed, which I had immediately crawled into as soon as Mom and I got home from lunch. "But I just can't do it." I shook my head. "Today, it's pictures blown up to poster-size. What's it going to be tomorrow?"

"Tuesday?" Alice asked.

"No. I mean, what will she stoop to doing *then*? Reading aloud from my diary?

"You didn't tell me you started keeping a diary!" Alice said. "Plus, how would she get it?"

I sighed. "Alice, I don't have one. I was just trying to make a point. All I'm saying is that with her, there's no telling what can happen." I turned. "Malia, because you're the new New Girl, you probably understand a lot better than these guys will. I'm sick of standing out. I just want to blend into the crowd for once."

Alice nodded. "It's a good thing your hair grew back, 'cause I bet you *really* stood out after the Hat Incident."

"Look, Alice, I know you're trying to help—" I started to say.

"But you're actually not," Beatrice said.

It may have seemed mean of Beatrice and me to say that, but Alice had lived in New York her whole life. She knew it was just standard tell-it-like-it-is New York–ese and therefore didn't get upset. Plus, we didn't say it meanly. "But what about all those art supplies we bought at the stationery store yesterday to make more posters?" Alice asked.

"And the second button maker?" Malia added.

"And the fact that we just spent money from our campaign fund so we could pay my cousin Mark in Hot Tamales for updating LucyB4Prez.com?" Beatrice asked.

"Lucy, someone has to stop Cristina," said Alice.

I shook my head. "I'm sorry, but someone else is going to have to do it," I said. "I'm retiring from my career in politics."

"But it hasn't actually started yet," said Malia.

"Yeah, well, it's an early, early retirement," I replied as I slid farther beneath the covers and started to pull them up over my head.

"But you were going to save the world," Alice said quietly. "You were going to make it a better, safer place for all the dorks."

"For everyone who has been teased because they're a little bit different," Malia said.

"For those who don't quite fit in, no matter how hard they try," Beatrice added.

I pulled the covers down a bit so I could get a peek at their faces before quickly pulling them up again. It was too sad. It was like the Petco adoption area and *Rescue Pets 911* times a hundred. "I'm sorry, guys. I tried," I said from underneath the covers. "I really did."

When no one said anything, I peeked out again. Which, the moment I did, I wish I hadn't.

Because the only thing worse than having a poster-size photo of your egghead splashed across the school walls is the sight of your friends looking at you with total disappointment in their eyes.

chapter 8

Dear Dr. Maude,

After I tell you what happened yesterday, you probably won't want to be friends with me anymore, so I just wanted to say it's been really nice knowing you. Even if you didn't answer any of my e-mails. Not even ONE.

It's kind of a long story, so I won't go into all of it now. Especially because every time I think about it—which is a lot—I burst into tears, and now my eyes are so swollen I can't see that well. The only good news is that I'm such a mess that even Miss Piggy feels bad for me. To the point where she let me hug her for an entire thirty-five seconds (I timed it) until she started hissing and trying to bite me.

Anyway, what it comes down to is, I have to drop out of the election. I haven't officially dropped out yet, because Mom let me stay home from school again today. Usually she has what she calls "zero tolerance" for my trying to get out of going to school, but this time she's being cool about it. But when I finally do go back to school—which I'm hoping won't be for another month—then I will officially drop out. By then the election will be over because voting is next Monday, but I think it's important to do things officially, you know?

The reason that I have to drop out is because Cristina Pollock is a horrible human being who will stop at nothing to get what she wants. Even if it means ruining other people's lives forever by showing photos of them where they look like eggheads.

But you want to know the worst part of all this, Dr. Maude? Even worse than knowing that all that time I spent practicing my "President Lucy B. Parker" signature was a complete waste of time, not to mention ink and paper? The worst part is seeing how disappointed my friends, and Mom, and Dad, and Alan, and Pete are in me. They don't actually say, "Wow, Lucy, I'm really disappointed in you" out loud, because they know if they did, I'd probably burst into tears, but I can feel it.

Luckily Laurel's been in Miami for some Save-the-Something-or-Other event, so I haven't had to deal with her reaction, too. If she didn't already think I'm a total loser (which I'm pretty sure she does), this would be the thing that did it. It's a good thing we're still not really talking because every time I just THINK about the idea of telling her what happened, I get so embarrassed that I pull the covers up over my head. Even if no one's in the room other than Miss Piggy.

Okay, well, it's time to get back to that. You'd think that because that's pretty much all I've been doing the last two days I'd be bored with it by now, but I'm not. Plus, when you're not around other human beings, you don't

147

have to worry about the fact that your hair is all greasy because you're too upset to wash it. Like I said, I totally don't blame you if you don't write me back. I wouldn't write me back, either.

I'm not even going to bother asking for advice because my life is so ruined, nothing could possibly make it better.

yours truly,
Lucy B. Parker

The thing about staying in bed pretty much nonstop for almost twenty-four hours is that your body gets all achy. And you get REALLY hungry because you're so bored. Which is why, after I sent the e-mail to Dr. Maude, I went to the kitchen in search of snacks.

Unfortunately, because of the boredom, I had eaten all the good snack stuff by that point and was now down to stuff like disgusting sunflower seeds.

I was in the middle of mixing them with the tiny bit of peanut butter that was left over from my earlier peanut-butter-and-Skittles snack when I heard the front door open.

"Oh great," I sighed. Mom and Alan were at therapy (separately, because their joint therapy session was on Fridays). They wouldn't be back for half an hour. And

Rose was in Jamaica visiting her family. So that meant Laurel was home.

And because one of the OCD things that she did as soon as she got home was to immediately wash her hands in the kitchen because that's where the extra-super-germ-killing antibacterial soap was kept, I could forget about crawling back under the covers without her seeing me.

"Hi," she said a little-bit-cold-but-not-entirely-frozen as she walked in and headed over to the sink.

"Hi," I mumbled, cringing as I looked down at Mom's old holey Smith College sweatshirt that I had managed to save from the Goodwill pile when she was first becoming the new New York version of herself.

She sniffed. "What's that smell?"

I lifted up my sweatshirt and sniffed. "Me," I said glumly. "I didn't have time to shower today." Because I was busy hiding under my covers.

When she was done washing her hands, she looked up at me. Her eyes widened. "Are you sick? You look awful! And the baby shower is this weekend—you can't go if you're sick!"

Right. The baby shower. Which, in light of everything that was going on, I wasn't letting myself think about because then I'd get only *more* depressed. I shook my head, afraid to open my mouth. The last thing I needed was to start to cry in front of her.

"Wait, it's only two o'clock. Why are you home from school?"

"I…there…" As much as I tried to stop it, I could feel my eyes start to fill.

She hurried over and grabbed me by the shoulders. "Lucy, tell me what's wrong!" she said, concerned.

I looked at her looking at me, all caring and big frister–like, not moving away from me even though I could tell by that point that I really *did* smell. The tears in my eyes began to plop down on my sweatshirt. Which I knew would make it smell even worse. "There was … an…an incident at school," I finally wailed.

"Oh no! What kind of incident? How big?" she asked. "Like a regular incident, or an Incident-with-a-capital-I?"

"More like an incident-in-all-caps!" I wailed even louder.

"Oh Lucy!" She grabbed me and hugged me tight, not even seeming to care about any sort of germs or dandruff that might have jumped off of me and onto her. Which was huge progress on her part, I knew. "It's okay," she said.

"No, actually, it's not!" I wailed again.

This was so weird. For the last twenty-four hours, as upset as I had been, I had managed to keep it together in front of people. But now that Laurel was here—the person who I had *thought* I had to hide the most in front of—I actually felt like I could finally let it all out.

"Can you tell me what happened?" she asked gently.

I nodded as I wiped my face with my sweatshirt.

"So . . . are you going to tell me?"

"I'm trying to!" I said, starting to cry again. "It's just that it takes a lot of energy to talk about something so humiliating!"

I sat down at the kitchen table and took a few deep breaths. Finally, I was able to calm down and tell her the story. Which was easier to do after I remembered the box of Thin Mints I had stashed away on the top-top shelf of the pantry.

"Oh wow. That's really awful," she said, munching away. "I guess the good news is that now it'll give you all the motivation you need to really go all out with the rest of your campaign."

I lifted my head up from the table and looked at her. "What rest of my campaign? I'm done."

"But Lucy, you can't give up now!"

What was wrong with these people? "Um, yeah, I can. And I am," I said firmly as I slithered down in my seat so only my chin was resting on the table. Because telling the story had brought on a whole new wave of embarrassment, all I wanted to do was hide.

She got up from the table and paced around the kitchen for a second before turning to me. "Go take a shower and get dressed."

"Why?" I asked suspiciously. If she was planning

on taking me over to Cristina's apartment and making us "communicate in a healthy and productive manner," which had been Alan's idea the night before, there was no way I was going.

"Because I want to tell you a story. But before I do, we need some supplies."

Forty-five minutes later, Laurel and I were sitting across from each other at the place where we had gone for our first real IBS when I had moved to New York: Billy's Bakery, down on Ninth Avenue in Chelsea. Luckily for everyone involved, I had taken a quick shower and traded in my smelly sweatshirt for my peach-colored DON'T BE MEAN TO NERDS T-shirt and favorite denim miniskirt. I was still too depressed to wash my hair, but my denim newsboy cap hid the grease.

Laurel knew that when I was really upset, the only thing that could make me feel better was a red velvet cupcake. But it couldn't be from Crumbs (too dry) or Magnolia Bakery (too heavy) or Buttercup Bake Shop (too small). In order to truly cheer me up, it had to come from Billy's. I'm not sure what super-top-secret special ingredient the people there put in their batter, but whatever it was, it had this way of completely shifting a person's attitude. When I mentioned that once to Mom, she said the special ingredient was probably just extra amounts of sugar, but I disagreed. I had tried eating sugar straight from the package, and instead of making me happy, it just made me sick. Although according to Beatrice, doing that *did* cure hiccups.

And the only thing better than one red velvet cupcake from Billy's was three of them—which is how many were sitting between us. As I looked at them I started to cry.

"But I thought you loved Billy's!" Laurel said anxiously. "I thought this would cheer you up!"

I sniffled. "No. It will! It's just . . . so awesome when your best friend knows you well enough to know that sometimes the only solution to your pain is a cupcake from your favorite bakery!"

At that, Laurel started to get all teary, too. Although, because she had her sunglasses on because she hadn't had time to put on a full-blown dork disguise, no one would have been able to see it but me. "I'm still your best friend? Really?"

I nodded.

"So you don't hate me anymore?"

"I never hated you," I replied. "I thought you hated me because I got all mad about you wanting to be involved in the campaign!"

"Well, I *was* hurt that you thought my ideas were stupid," she admitted.

"I didn't think they were stupid at all!" I replied. "I just . . . it was really important that if I went through with this, that I was doing it as *me*. As Lucy. And not as your unfamous little frister. I didn't want people voting for me because they thought that if they did, they'd get to meet you."

She nodded. "I get it."

I sighed. "But now they're not going to be voting for me at all, especially because I'm dropping out, so it doesn't matter."

She scooted her chair around so that the two girls sitting at the table behind us couldn't see her face and start going nuts once they figured out who she was. Even with the sunglasses, her blonde hair sometimes gave her away.

"But wait—I haven't told you my story yet."

I used a plastic knife to cut the third cupcake in half and took my part. Granted it was a little bigger than the other half, but because of how upset I was, I figured Laurel would understand.

"Did I ever tell you about the day I went in for the Fruity Cocoa Crunchy Pebbles audition?" she asked.

"That commercial you did when you were five?" I asked.

She nodded. "Yeah. It was my first commercial. The whole week leading up to the audition, I was really excited," she said. "I kept practicing my lines. Well, my *line*. There was only one." She put her hands on her hips and cocked her head. "'Fruity Cocoa Crunchy Pebbles sure are yummy!'" she announced in a very kidlike, commercial-y voice.

"That's really good," I said.

"Thanks. Anyway, then the morning of the audition, before my mom and I were going to drive into the city from New Jersey, I started to totally panic. And I hid under the bed. For like an hour."

"You did? But you hate small, dark spaces," I said. "Almost as much as you hate germs. They give you hives."

She nodded. "Exactly," she said. "So after looking for me all over the house, my mom came into my room and saw my pink sneaker under the bed and told me to come out, and when I wouldn't, she had to crouch down and slide underneath the bed, too. But she got *stuck*."

I gasped. "She did?" Wow. This was almost as good as a *telenovela*.

"Yup. So because she was stuck, I was stuck, too. Even if I wanted to get out, I couldn't," she said. "She shifted around to try to find a way to get unstuck, and asked me what was wrong. I told her that I didn't want to go to the audition because what if I screwed up my line on national TV and everyone in America saw it."

"And then what happened?" I asked excitedly. Laurel was a really good storyteller. Especially the way she left just the right amount of pause time between sentences so that you were just dying to hear what came next.

"So she explained how an audition is just an audition. You haven't been chosen yet, so the only people who are seeing it are the people in the room like the director and the casting director and it's not actually on TV," Laurel said. "That made me feel a little better. But it was what she said next that was the thing that really changed my mind."

"She said that if you guys didn't figure out how to get out from under the bed, you'd suffocate and die from lack of air?" I suggested breathlessly.

"No. Although I do remember I was starting to get kind of woozy." She leaned in and grabbed my arm. "What she said was that heroes weren't heroes because they weren't afraid," she whispered. "They were heroes because they had *courage*, which meant that even though they were afraid, they didn't let that stop them. They did whatever it was they needed to do anyway."

Huh. I liked that. It was catchy. In fact, it was so catchy, it would have been a great thing to use in one of my State of the Grade addresses, had I been elected president. Which would not be happening because of the I-was-just-so-humiliated-I-have-to-drop-out thing.

"And then she said that if I didn't show up for the audition, I'd never know whether I would have gotten it or not. And if I never knew whether I would have gotten it or not, I'd never know whether I was any good at commercials. And if I never knew if I was any good at commercials, then I'd probably never get an audition for a movie or a TV show, and if I never—"

The thing was, sometimes when Laurel was telling a story, she tended to go on and on. "Okay—you can stop now. I get the picture," I said.

She whipped off her sunglasses and grabbed my hand. Luckily, the girls had already left. "Lucy, now is not the time to quit. Now is the time to call on the heroness inside of you!"

Was *heroness* even a word? Maybe it was like my Lucyness, which is something that Mom always brought up even though I had no idea what she was talking about.

"If you let fear get in your way and you just give up," she went on, "you won't be able to serve as an example of what can happen if you feel the fear but do it anyway."

She was right . . . and if this had been a Very Special episode of *Madison*, now would be the time I jumped up and said, "You're right!" But this wasn't a Very Special episode of some TV show. It was my life.

"Nice try, Laurel, but no," I said.

"Lucy, you have an opportunity that very few people in the world get. The opportunity to be a *role model*. A role model for everyone who isn't popular, or who is considered a little weird because they keep period logs and—"

"Wait—I keep period logs. You think I'm weird?"

"No. *I* don't think you're weird, but some other people might find that a little weird."

I shrugged. Well, those people were stupid because anyone with half a brain would know that being able to see where you fell in the whole period situation compared to your classmates was very important.

"You're a role model because you show people that normal girls are just as cool and just as special as popular ones," she said.

"Or famous ones?" I asked quietly.

She smiled. "Yes. Just as cool as famous ones," she replied. "Come on, you know that no matter how many 'Coolest Celeb' gossip-blog polls I win, I totally don't believe any of it." That was true—she didn't. "I mean, as far as I'm concerned, I am so *not* cool."

I shrugged. "Well, I think you're the coolest," I said. The whole love-of-organizing, and alphabetizing, and Purelling once an hour may not have been cool, but when it came to big-frister things like believing in me and giving me pep talks, she was the best. "So what happened with the bed?"

"Huh?"

"You and your mom. Stuck under the bed before the audition. Without any air."

"Oh that. Well, she sucked all her breath in so she got a little flatter and was able to wriggle out and then I got out.

We went to the audition and even though by that time we were late and they had just finished seeing the last person, Mom convinced them to let me go in. I got the gig and then a month after that I got a guest role on *F.B.I. Newark* and the casting director of that was best friends with the casting director over at Kidz TV and then I got *Madison*."

"Wow. So that bravery thing really paid off," I said, impressed.

"I guess so," she agreed. "So you'll keep going with the election?"

I thought about it. Was it bravery that kept a person in the race after being completely humiliated, or was it just plain stupidity? I wasn't sure. But what I *was* sure about was that if I was going to keep going, I would need some help.

"Okay," I finally said. "But under one condition."

As soon as we got home, I called an official emergency campaign meeting for after dinner.

"You do know that the season premiere of *America's Worst Dancers* is on right now, don't you?" Beatrice asked as she walked into my room and flopped down on my bed. That was her favorite show.

"Not to mention *An Insider's Inside Look Behind the Scenes of the Real Eighth Graders of San Francisco*," added Alice.

"I know, I know—I'm TiVoing them right now. We can watch them after," I said.

"Did you happen to TiVo the PBS special about the oldest-living tree?" Malia asked excitedly. "Because I spaced and forgot."

"Uh, no," I said. "Sorry." I liked Malia a lot, but she had awful taste in TV programs.

"So what's so important that you had to call this special emergency meeting?" Alice asked. "I thought you were going to quit the race."

"Yeah," Malia said. "Once you finally come back to school."

"There's been a change of plans," I replied as I walked over to my bathroom. "I'm going to go through with it."

"You are?" Beatrice asked, impressed.

"Really?" Malia asked excitedly. "What made you change your mind?"

"A conversation I had with an old friend," I replied.

"Can I be the one to videotape you casting your vote?" Alice asked. "Because I've been practicing with my camera, and I've gotten a lot better at it."

"Huh. I can't decide if that's totally brave . . . or totally nuts," Beatrice said.

I rolled my eyes. "Have-Nots, I'd like to introduce you to the newest member of our team," I announced excitedly, flinging the door open.

"How is a cat going to help us?" Beatrice asked, confused.

I looked down to see Miss Piggy waddling out before plopping down on the rug and starting to groom herself. "Not her," I said. I leaned my head into the bathroom. "It's your cue," I whispered. A second later, Laurel came out wearing a Have-Not T-shirt with a Lucy B. for Prez! button pinned over her heart.

I walked over to my desk and picked up the campaign rules and regulations I had downloaded and printed out. "Now, as you guys know, the election is Monday, and final speeches are tomorrow. Our only chance at winning would be if I gave a completely awesome speech tomorrow."

"No offense, Lucy, but if it's like the one you gave a few weeks ago, we're in big trouble," Alice said.

"Yeah, I know. Which is why I'm not going to give one." I turned to Laurel. "She is."

"But she's not running—you are," said Alice, confused.

I held up the rules and regulations. "Yeah, but nowhere in here does it say that the person running has to be the one giving the speech."

Beatrice grabbed them from me. "Let me see those." She looked them over. "You're right—it doesn't."

"So if that's the case," I went on, "why not have someone who's used to giving speeches in front of thousands of people do it?"

They all looked at one another. "Okay, *now* you're talking big-city ideas," said Beatrice. "That's genius!"

"But what about . . . you know," Alice said.

"What's 'you know'?" I asked.

She nodded her head toward Laurel. "That whole thing about how you didn't want to ask . . . *someone* . . . for help because of the f-a-m-o-u-s thing," she whispered. However, because Alice was Alice, the whisper was closer to a yell.

"It's okay. I was thinking about it, and I know that I am who I am. And it doesn't matter how I win at this point. It's what I do after I win that's the important part," I replied. I ran over to my closet and reached for a bag of tortilla chips and a jar of salsa I had smuggled in from the kitchen. "Now, everyone get comfortable. We've got work to do."

chapter 9

Dear Dr. Maude,

Guess where I am? If you guessed "hiding in the girls' room," you'd be right. I know, by now you probably think I'm pretty weird, but if YOUR future was about to be decided in ten minutes—actually, I take that back . . . EIGHT minutes!— YOU'D be freaking out, too.

Okay, maybe because you're you, you wouldn't be (BTW, my mom loved your book *Get It Together Already, People: Ten Foolproof Ways to Calm Yourself Down That Will Work Even If You Are a Fool)*. But because I don't have as much life experience as you do, I am freaking out. A lot.

It's kind of a long story, so I won't go into all of it now, but basically all you need to know is this: Not only are Laurel and I friends again, but I decided not to drop out of the campaign. AND I asked her to be part of it. Sure, maybe some people— or a lot of them—might vote for me just because she and I live together, but you know what? That's fine. Because it's what I do AFTER I win that really matters.

If for some reason you do end up reading this in the next few minutes, please wish me luck. Or rather, wish Laurel luck, because she's the one who's about to give a speech about me. But if you don't end up reading it until this weekend, you can still wish me luck because (a) the baby shower for Ziggy is this weekend and (b) the actual voting part of the election isn't until Monday. After Monday, I won't need it. I mean, I WILL need it, but I won't.... I think you get my point.

yours truly,
LUCY B. PARKER

If there was ever a day that I was glad we had worked on coming up with good disguises for Laurel, it was today. With Laurel dressed in a long plaid skirt with a buttoned-up white blouse with frilly lace collar, ugly brown loafers, a short, blechy brown bob wig, and thick black-rimmed glasses, Alice and I had no problem sneaking her through the halls and hiding her in the janitor's closet until it was time for the assembly. If anyone did look at her, it was with confusion, as if they were trying to figure out if she was an Amish exchange student.

The plan was that soon after the assembly started, Malia would say that she needed to go to the bathroom and would go get Laurel, who would then change into her normal clothes. After that, Malia would sneak her in through the back of the auditorium to where I was waiting backstage.

I stood there, listening to Cristina give her speech about how excited she was to be president again, and how she was sorry she hadn't gotten to meet as many unpopular kids during the campaign as she would have liked. I couldn't believe how calm I was. Usually none of my plans worked out the way they were supposed to, but this one was going off without a hitch. So far, at least.

There wasn't a ton of laughter or clapping for Cristina. No text from Laurel saying she was having a panic attack in the janitor's closet because of her claustrophobia. No sweat stains underneath my arms.

If it weren't for the baby shower that I'd be leaving for in a few hours, I could say that life was actually . . . really good.

Well, until I turned around and saw Laurel. And the fact that she was still in her dorky disguise.

"Why are you still wearing that?" I hissed.

"Alice left the wrong bag with me. And then I texted you, but you didn't reply," Laurel whispered as she pushed her fake glasses up on the bridge of her nose.

"I didn't get a text from you!" I said as I took my phone out. Which, I discovered, I had somehow managed to turn off. When I turned it on, there was Laurel's text. As well as one that said, *Uh-oh. I just realized I left the wrong bag with Laurel* . . . from Alice.

I sighed. That was the problem when people copied celebrities by buying the things they saw them with in magazines—Alice and Laurel had the same pink I'M NOT A PAPER BAG AND I'M PROUD OF IT tote.

I walked over to the curtain and peered behind it. As Cristina said, "Well, I'm going to wrap it up now. I mean, what more can I say other than if you're smart, you'll vote for me because . . . well, I'm me," I looked back at Laurel pacing in her dork outfit and started to panic.

"This is a disaster!" I cried, flopping down in a chair. I put my head between my knees, a trick Laurel had taught me. She did it whenever she got super-anxious. Like, say, when she had to sing at the White House. "What are we going to do now?"

Laurel, whose brown loafers made a very annoying *squeak/squish/creak* sound, stopped pacing and turned to me. "Actually, it's not a disaster," she said calmly. "In fact, it's perfect."

I lifted my head up. "Um, how is this perfect?"

"Thank you for that very . . . self-confident speech, Cristina," I heard Dr. Rem-Wall say into the microphone. "And now, we'll hear from her opponent—Lucy B. Parker." I tried not to cringe at the lame amount of applause that followed.

Laurel smoothed her wig and walked over to the curtain. Before she lifted it, she turned to me. "Season three, episode five," she said, then disappeared through it.

"What does *that* mean?!" I cried. I didn't even have Internet access so I could look it up on the online episode guide on the *Madison* website. This couldn't get any worse!

I ran over to the edge of the stage so I could watch things go even more wrong than they already were. I peeked out at the crowd and heard them start to whisper once they got a look at someone who obviously wasn't me. Very quickly, the whispers turned to giggles.

"Good afternoon, students of the Center for Creative Learning," Laurel said into the microphone. "As you can see, I'm not Lucy B. Parker—"

"Yeah, you're even dorkier than she is!" Mark Wallace yelled out. I had always thought he was a jerk, but now I *knew* he was.

Beatrice stood up from her seat in the front room and whipped around. "Excuse me, *you're* calling someone a dork?"

I cringed. As awesome as it was that Beatrice had the guts to stand up in front of the entire seventh grade on my behalf, this was not the time for a debate about whether I was a dork or not to take place.

"Yeah, who *are* you?" Renata Spencer called out. "Because I don't think I've ever seen you before."

"Are you Amish?" someone else called out.

Cristina stood up and turned toward the crowd. "I'd just like to say that whoever she is, to show how committed I am to this school, I'm more than happy to completely make her over after this assembly is over. I know one of Lucy's campaign slogans was friends don't let friends be mean to dorks, but as far as I'm concerned, friends also don't let friends walk around looking like that." The crowd laughed. "At least let me try and do something with your hair."

Just as I was about to rush onto the stage and rescue Laurel, she reached up and yanked off her wig. "You mean something more like this?" she asked sweetly when the audience gasped.

I really wished I'd had my camera with me, because the sight of Cristina looking like a bug-eyed blowfish with her mouth stuck in the shape of an *O* was beyond awesome.

The audience began to buzz, and Laurel reached up and, with a big smile, calmly removed her glasses. "So as I was saying," she went on, "I'm not Lucy B. Parker. I'm her big frister, Laurel."

The crowd began to whisper. "We love you, Laurel Moses!" Samantha Pringle yelled out. According to her Facebook profile, Samantha was the four-time president of the Gramercy Park chapter of the Laurel Moses Fan Club.

"Wow," Laurel said. "That's *soooo* sweet of you guys!"

Okay, I was officially lost. What was going on here?

And why was she being so nice to people who had just been so mean to her? I mean, yes, Laurel was a genuinely nice person; and because she was a superstar, she had to be a lot more careful than normal people not to lose her temper or else it would end up as front-page news, but still—this was not how I'd expected this to go.

Laurel's smile started to fade. "But I have to say, I'm a little confused," she continued. "'Cause a second ago, before you knew it was me, when you thought I was this dorky . . . Amish person, you didn't seem to love me."

"Of course we do," Cristina sputtered. "See, we were just *acting*."

"Oh. You mean how some of you *act* like non-popular people aren't as important as popular ones?" She shrugged. "Because I doubt that anyone in this school really feels that way. Right?"

Was it my imagination, or did Cristina turn bright red?

"You know, as horrible as it felt to stand up on this stage and be made fun of, I'm glad it happened," Laurel went on. "Because that, more than anything, shows you why Lucy's promise to end dork discrimination and get rid of Mean People–ism is so important."

Ohhhh . . . Now I remembered season three, episode five! It was the one where Madison got mad that girls weren't allowed to join the football team, and disguised herself as a boy and tried out and then, after her true identity was discovered, gave this big speech about how everyone was created equal.

Cristina stood up and turned to Dr. Rem-Wall. "Excuse me, but the *candidates* are supposed to be giving these speeches. Not their family members or friends. This is against the rules!"

I walked out from behind the curtain. "Actually, if you look in the rules and regulations, you'll see that it doesn't say who has to give the second speech." I handed my printout to Dr. Rem-Wall. "You can double-check, if you'd like."

She took the paper from me and looked it over. "Lucy seems to be right, Cristina. Now please sit down. And be quiet."

Led by Beatrice, the members of Team Have-Not stood up and clapped. It was a little sad, the sight of three lone figures in that big crowd, but it still made me all teary. Mom was always saying that you were super lucky to go through life with just one good friend, so the fact that I had four made me way above average. Which Alan would be happy about, seeing that he was always going on about how, to get into a good college, you had to be beyond average.

"I know a lot of you don't know Lucy that well because she only moved to New York last spring. I just want you to know that those of you who haven't had a chance to spend time with her, you're really missing out," Laurel went on. "I've been lucky to meet a lot of interesting people in my life, but I'm here to tell you that Lucy's at the top of the list."

"Even more interesting than Austin Mackenzie?" someone called out.

She smiled. "Yeah. Even more interesting than Austin. And if any of you read the gossip blogs, you know that I find him pretty interesting."

Everyone laughed, including me. Maybe this wasn't a total disaster after all.

"But what's even cooler than her hat collection, or the fact that she has more pairs of Chuck Taylors than anyone I know, or that she keeps a lot of logs, is the fact that more than anyone I know, Lucy is one hundred percent herself," she said. "If she tells you she's going to do something, she does it. If she tells you she likes your outfit, she means it. Unfortunately, if you ask her if your outfit looks stupid, and she says yes, you have to believe that, too." More laughter. "And if I went to a regular school instead of being tutored on set, I'd totally want a president like that."

I was glad to see the nodding that was coming from the audience.

"I'd want a president who knows what it's like *not* to be popular!" she continued. "Who knows what it's like to be teased!" A chorus of "mm-hm"s could be heard. "To understand the pain of what it's like to be chosen last for volleyball for gym!"

"I know what that feels like!" cried Fred Dresser, a freckled-faced, shrimpy, chosen-last-in-gym kid.

Wow. Maybe Laurel should give up acting and go into politics. She was *really* good at this.

"To . . . to . . . to be made to wait for an hour in a very hot monkey costume so you get super-sweaty and look disgusting when the camera starts rolling and you have to take it off because the guest star on that week's episode of your series thinks you were flirting with her boyfriend which, by the way, you totally were not."

Okay, maybe that part got her a lot of confused looks, but she really had them up until then.

"You guys don't have the honor of living with Lucy B. Parker, but I do," she said passionately. "And I'm here to tell you that she's got what it takes to make it so that instead of there being Haves and Have-Nots, *everyone* is a Have! And all of those lines that keep us from getting along—whether they're visible or invisible—will be erased! And the world— or at least the seventh grade at the Center for Creative Learning—will be a much happier, much more peaceful place!"

At that, the entire crowd except for Cristina Pollock

got to their feet and cheered. Even Tweedle Dee and Tweedle Dumber got swept up in Laurel's inspiring message of hope. Although she was standing kind of far away from me, I could have sworn that Marni had tears in her eyes. Even *I* believed how awesome I was after that speech.

"And I just want to say one more thing before I go," Laurel added. "I really hope that when you cast your votes on Monday, if you vote for Lucy, it's because you believe in her. And not just because a person who happens to be lucky enough to have her own TV show says you should."

Although I had been biting the inside of my cheek to stop myself from crying, I lost it at that. Laurel really did know me better than anyone.

"Because part of the Have/Have-Not problem is that too many times kids do something because a *Have* says that it's cool and not because *they* really want to. And I have a feeling that if you elect Lucy B. Parker for president, one of the best things that could come out of it is that you'll soon find that you'll be a little less scared to follow your heart."

Laurel turned around and walked toward me and grabbed my hand and dragged me to the center of the stage. "*This* is who you want for president, you guys!" she cried, holding my hand up.

I didn't even care that by that time, tears were rolling

down my face. I just let them. Just like I didn't even care if I won the election. Because to be no longer fighting with Laurel, and to hear her say the things she had just said in front of a huge auditorium of people—that was worth more than anything in the world.

chapter 10

Dear Dr. Maude,

Here's a question for you: How on earth is a person supposed to get through forty-eight hours of nervousness without (a) throwing up or (b) saying every two seconds, "Oh my God, I'm SO nervous," to the point where the person's mother says, "Lucy, honey, I understand that you're nervous about the election on Monday, but you're going to have to calm down. Or at least stop announcing it every two seconds, because it's driving me crazy"?

As you know, before Laurel's speech on Friday afternoon, I pretty much thought the election was a lost cause. Even after the speech, I thought she'd be mobbed by everyone while I just stood there feeling like a Frister of. But that's not what happened. A bunch of kids came up to me and said that while they had been on the fence up until then as to who to vote for, they realized that I was the better candidate! Not to jinx it or anything, but I think I might have a shot at winning this thing.

I'm not sure if you're a religious person or anything (I looked on your website, but it doesn't say), but if you wouldn't mind saying a prayer or two or fifteen between now and Monday, I'd really appreciate it.

yours truly,
Lucy B. Parker

P.S. I was just thinking that because you never answered my e-mail about whether you would mind doing a video for me saying that you thought I'd be make a good president, the praying could make up for that.

After the speech, Mom picked me up at school so we could head up to Northampton for the shower. Once I finally stopped babbling in the car about how awesome Laurel's speech had been, and how she was the best frister in the entire world, Mom turned off the radio.

I cringed. If she was going to use the car ride up as the opportunity for another "check-in," I was going to go nuts.

"Honey, I wanted to check in, and see how you're feeling about your dad."

I sighed. Yup, she was. "Fine," I replied.

She shook her head. "Lucy, 'fine' is not a good enough answer in this case. I think you're having feelings."

This was too much. "Why do you think that just because I'm a twelve-year-old girl I'm always having feelings?" I cried.

"Because that's a twelve-year-old girl's *job*," she replied. "Now, I know your dad hasn't been as sensitive to them as he usually is, but soon enough Ziggy is going to be here, and I think you need to come to terms with that so that you're not projecting your anger and envy onto him. It's not fair. And I'd hate to see it ruin a really lovely occasion like this baby shower."

I wasn't quite sure what "projecting" meant, but I could tell from the tone of Mom's voice that what she was basically saying was, "You better stop it already, or else TV time is going to be taken away."

It's not like I wanted divorced parents who hated each other, but parents like mine who were still so close that one of them went to the other's baby shower and was *excited* about it? I'm sorry, but that was a little weird.

"You know, I was thinking, and I feel like you're doing the very thing that you're so passionately against." Mom said.

"What's that?"

"Discrimination."

"Who am I discriminating against?" I asked, confused.

"Against Ziggy," she replied. "He's not even born, and you don't even know him yet, but you've already come to the conclusion that he's boring. And whiny. And annoying."

"Yeah, well, he's a *baby*," I replied. "Everyone knows that's how they are."

She shrugged. "Huh. That's funny, because *you* weren't like that."

I looked at her. "I wasn't?"

She shook her head. "Nope. You were a great baby. Very mellow," she said. "You barely cried, and you spent most of your time just sort of taking everything in. Everyone was always commenting on how easy you were."

I smiled. I hadn't known that. That was pretty cool. I wonder if that was something to put on my campaign website.

"Except for the fact that you had a lot of gas," she added.

I cringed. Okay, that part I didn't need to know. And neither did voters.

She laughed. "It was so cute. You'd be sitting there and then these tiny little farts would come out—"

"Okay, Mom—I get it. You can stop now," I said, turning red.

"Anyway, the way you talk about Ziggy, it seems to me to have a little bit of . . . baby discrimination about it," she said. "And if you think about it, babies and dorks have a lot in common. Like the fact that they both have trouble standing up for themselves. Which makes it an unfair fight."

I thought about it. She wasn't wrong. Babies and dorks *did* have a lot in common.

"And I know that someone like yourself who feels so passionately about wanting to end dork discrimination would never want to be seen as discriminating against any sort of minority..."

That was true, too. And not just because I was running for president and wanted votes. I really *did* feel strongly that all people were created equal. And I guess because babies were technically people, even though they were still babies, they were included as well.

She shrugged again. "Just something to think about," she said as she reached for the radio and turned on some Joni Mitchell.

As if I didn't have *enough* rolling around in my head already.

If I was going to try my best not to discriminate against anyone, I guess "weird yoga people" fell into that category, too.

But as I found out at the baby shower, when you're forced to be around thirty of them, it's very, very hard. Not only that, but if the mother of the baby-to-be has made all of them remove their shoes because she doesn't want the house being contaminated with other people's karma, it's also very stinky.

Meeting Sarah's mother, Astrid, explained a lot. Dad

had mentioned that she was "truly one of a kind" (Dad-ese for "pretty weird"), but he had left off the fact that she was completely *nuts*.

"Astrid is a very pretty name," I said as we sat together on the couch eating our *naan* and *raita*. *Naan* is this really yummy Indian bread, and *raita* is this yogurt and cucumber stuff you dipped it in. Because of Alan's sensitive stomach, we didn't get to eat Indian food all that often at home, and I really missed it. Although the fact that there was a yoga teacher twisting himself into a pretzel-like shape on the floor four feet in front of me was kind of taking away my appetite.

"Thank you," she said, readjusting the turban on her head. I had worn a turban once—to a movie premiere in L.A.—but it wasn't by *choice*, like she was doing. It was only because my hair happened to have turned blue minutes before we were supposed to leave. "My birth name is Betty, but on one of my spiritual pilgrimages in India, an astrologer there suggested I change it to Astrid in order to more accurately fulfill my destiny."

I waited for the "Just kidding" part, but it didn't come. "Oh. Well, that's cool," I said. "So, um, Sarah said you live in Arizona?"

She nodded. "Yes. I worked on Wall Street for a long time, but then I had a nervous breakdown," she replied. "Luckily, I had made enough money in the stock market before the economy collapsed not to have to work anymore. So when my psychic suggested I move to Sedona because the energy vortexes would have a healing effect on me, I packed up and was there the following week."

I didn't know what an energy vortex was, and, to be honest, I didn't want to. I looked around for Mom so that she could save me, but she was too busy talking to Mathieu and Manfred, the couple who owned the cheese store underneath Dad's old studio.

Astrid sighed. "But since the Spacecraft Incident, I'm seriously thinking of moving."

I put my naan down and stared at her. "*Spacecraft* Incident?" Incidents didn't have to do with spacecrafts. They had to do with things like hats. And posters.

"Yes," she said. "One of them hit the side of my house last month. Left a huge dent in the garage door. Unfortunately, my homeowner's insurance doesn't cover extraterrestrial damage, so it cost me a bundle to repair it."

Okay, now she was starting to scare me. I waited for the "This time I'm *really* just kidding," but instead she just smiled sweetly. Wow. If even the tiniest bit of that was remotely true, that was a serious Incident-with-a-capital-I.

I stood up. "Would you excuse me for a moment? I have to . . . go do something. It was nice talking to you."

Before she could say anything, I ran over to Mom.

"Hi, sweetie. Why don't you talk to Mathieu and Manfred while I run to the bathroom," she said.

"Uh . . . okay." It may have been because they were

from Europe (Mathieu was French and Manfred was German), and therefore their idea of being nice was different from the American way of being nice, but I had always found them kind of snotty. I mean, if you put out free samples of cheese for people to take and you only want them to take one, then you should put a sign up that says PLEASE TAKE ONE. But if there's no sign, how is a person supposed to know that five is too many?

"So, Lucy, you are about to be a big sister, *ja*?" asked Manfred.

I nodded. "*Ja*. I mean, yes."

"Little babies, they are so . . . *babyish*," Mathieu clucked. The way he said it made it sound like that definitely wasn't a good thing. But that also may have been the French thing.

I shrugged. "I guess so. But, I mean, they're sort of supposed to be, right?"

"Yes, but that is the *problem*," he sighed. "The way they cannot do anything for themselves. And have to eat all day long instead of waiting until the normal dinnertime of nine o'clock," he complained. That must have been a French thing, too, because nine o'clock was way late to eat dinner in America.

"I think that's because they're growing and stuff," I replied. "And they have really little mouths, kind of like birds, so it's not like they can eat as much as we can all at once." I wasn't sure if that was true, but it sounded good.

"Yes, but then there is the *crying*," Manfred added, rolling his eyes. "All the time with the crying! Even in public."

Okay, this was getting a little unfair. "Well, if I didn't know how to talk and tell someone what was wrong, I'd get annoyed, too," I replied.

"And the way they grow out of their expensive little outfits so fast!" Mathieu clucked. "So . . . *rude* to the person who bought it, don't you think?" He turned to Manfred. "I am so glad both of us do not like children."

Yeah, I was glad, too. Because it would have been miserable growing up with them. "You know, it's not like they *mean* to be annoying," I said defensively. "They're just little babies. And everyone around them is bigger than them and they have no say in anything. That's a horrible way to live."

Wait a minute—what if these guys were mean to Ziggy? I'd have to make sure to tell Dad about this so he could keep an extra-special eye out for them. Someone would have to, seeing that I wouldn't be here to do it. In fact, I'd go tell him right now.

"Excuse me, please," I said, walking over to the other side of the room where Dad was talking to his friends Nils and Francesca. They were photographers as well. But unlike Dad, who, when money was tight and he didn't have a gallery show coming up, would sometimes take pictures of kids and weddings, Nils and Francesca were what Mom called Artists-with-a-capital-A. Every time she said it, she rolled her eyes, so I don't think it was a compliment.

Nils was from Sweden and was pasty white with really blond hair that he didn't wash all that often. I didn't like to be near him too long because (a) he smelled like fish, and (b) he barely ever talked, which tended to make me start bloversharing and saying stupid things just to fill the silence.

Francesca, on the other hand, talked *all* the time. It was more like she complained—about everything. About the government; about the weather; about how reality TV was rotting people's brains (I bet if she watched stuff on Animal Planet she'd take that back). But mostly she complained about Nils and how depressed he was—right in front of him!

Dad looked up from the photographs he was showing them. "Hi, Monkey!" He smiled.

"Hi," I said. The Monkey thing was a little embarrassing, but because I had once heard Mom say during an overlistening session that if it didn't have to do with them, Nils and Francesca weren't paying attention, I didn't worry about it too much.

Francesca grabbed Dad's arm. "Oh, Brian," she gasped, "this one is just *stunning*. The *lighting*. The *composition*. The way the sun hits her nipples—"

At the word *nipples*, my eyebrows shot up so high I was afraid they had jumped off my face.

Francesca turned the photo toward me so I could see it. "Lucy, how does it feel to have such a talented father?"

Oh. My. God.

It was a picture of Sarah lying on the window seat in front of the big bay window that faced the front yard without any clothes on. *Nothing.* And you could see *everything.* Not just her ginormous stomach but everything *below* there, too.

This wasn't art with or without a capital A—this was just . . . *gross!* What was wrong with my father?! The only good thing was that soon enough I wouldn't be the only person embarrassed by him. Maybe with a sibling, it wouldn't be as humiliating because the embarrassing part would be cut in half.

"I'm so glad you like it, Francesca," said Dad. "Because it's such a special time in our lives, I really wanted to capture it on film."

"You know, you really should do more nudes," Francesca went on. "Not everyone is good at them, but you bring such a sense of *sensitivity* to them."

"Thanks, Francesca," said Dad, pleased. "That means a lot coming from you. I do like shooting the human form a lot more than a bowl of fruit . . ."

At least an apple or a bowl of grapes weren't disgusting and couldn't *embarrass* a person to death.

Nils stood there stroking his goatee. After clearing his throat a few times, he finally spoke. "This photo . . . it . . . it—"

We all leaned in closer so we could hear him.

"It...pierces my soul at its very core," he whispered.

Oh brother. I don't know why they thought Sarah looked so good. If you asked me, she kind of sort of looked like this whale I had seen on the news the other night that had washed up on a beach in New Jersey.

They went back to oohing and aahing over the photo and used the word *nipples* way too many times when the front door opened and Marissa and Cassandra walked in. I never thought the day would come where I would consider Marissa normal, but at that point I was *beyond* happy to see her.

"So were you able to find a baby to practice holding?" Marissa asked a little later as we stood in the corner and ate our sugar-free, wheat-free, flour-free, taste-free cake (Sarah may have been addicted to Tastykakes, but the other yoga guests weren't) while two women next to us talked about the best essential oil to help you lose weight.

"No," I said as I looked away from the guy doing a headstand across from me. His hairy belly was totally going to take away my appetite for the sundae I was going to force Mom into letting me get when this thing was over for being such a good sport about having to sit through it. "I've been too busy with the election. Plus, I still have time to learn. The baby won't be here for another three weeks."

"But what if Sarah ends up having the baby this weekend?" Cassandra asked. "Then what'll you do? Say you can't hold it because you're afraid you'll drop it?"

It was bad enough that Marissa had invited herself to the shower ("Because I'm going to be his babysitter, he needs to get used to me being around!"), but the fact that she had gotten Dad to say she could bring Cassandra? ("BFFs go everywhere together!") That was just wrong.

"She's not going to have the baby this weekend," I assured her. "Sure sometimes people have them like a few days early, but not, you know, *weeks* early."

"That's not true. I was born an entire *month* early," Marissa announced dramatically. "They had me on all these special machines and everything. According to my mom, it was *very* dramatic."

"And I was born three and a half weeks early," Cassandra added.

"Well, that's not going to happen here," I said nervously. The election was on Monday. The universe wouldn't be so cruel as to make it so that one of the most important events of my life would be totally pushed aside because Ziggy wasn't smart enough to know that it was a lot safer inside of Sarah's stomach than out here in the world. Or if he wanted to try to show me who was boss by taking up all the attention immediately.

Right?

chapter 11

Dear Dr. Maude,

Right now I'm SUPPOSED to be in the car with Mom driving back to New York.

But I'm not.

Instead it's eleven a.m. on Sunday, and I'm sitting on Dad's couch, waiting for Sarah's water to break so she can finally get in the bathtub and have this baby already. Which, according to Dad, isn't going to happen anytime soon because her contractions (Mom says they feel like period cramps) aren't very close together. Not only that, but I've been up since five because that's when he woke me to say that this whole giving-birth business had started. I don't know if I ever mentioned this to you, but I am NOT a morning person.

Dr. Maude, yesterday I felt like even though he's not born yet, Ziggy and I had managed to bond a little. I was even going to stick up for him if anyone baby discriminated against him. But now? After pulling this arriving-three-weeks-early-when-he-KNOWS-his

-older-sister-has-an-election-tomorrow-because-last
-night-she-bent-down-and-whispered-it-to-Sarah's-
belly business?

Not so much.

yours truly,
LUCY B. Parker

"How long did you say you were in labor with me again
after your water broke?" I asked Mom as we started what
had to be our tenth game of Go Fish. Movies and TV
shows always made giving birth look super-exciting
and dramatic, but as far as I was concerned, it was more
boring than algebra class.

"Thirty-five," she replied.

Phew. "Thirty-five minutes is nothing," I said, relieved.
I looked at my watch. "Even if we stay and hang out for
an hour after that, we'll still be home by dinnertime."

"Thirty-five *hours*," she corrected.

My face fell. Okay, thirty-five hours was not good. In
fact, thirty-five hours was very, very bad.

Not wanting to sound like a mean, horrible person,
I didn't dare bring up the idea that we weren't the ones
having the baby and didn't have to stay here. And because
Sarah already had a midwife and a doula and Astrid to

help her—not to mention Dad, even if from the way she was snapping at him just to get out of the way meant he wasn't being all that useful—they probably wouldn't mind if we went home.

Mom reached for my hand. "I think it's so wonderful that it worked out that you could be here for your brother's birth," she said as she squeezed it. "I think it will make you feel even closer to him. Maybe they'll let you cut the umbilical cord."

The idea of just *seeing* an umbilical cord let alone *cutting* it was beyond disgusting. "So . . . we're going to just hang out here doing nothing for the next thirty-five hours?" I asked. *When I could be back home getting ready for one of the most important days of my life?* I wanted to add, but didn't.

"We don't know if it'll take thirty-five hours," Mom said. "It could be a lot less."

I looked at my watch again. What if I won and had to give an acceptance speech? I'd have to practice it, and that would take time, and help from Team Have-Not. I wondered if I'd be lucky enough for Ziggy to take only the next fifteen minutes to be born.

Finally, THREE hours later, around one o'clock, when Sarah was five centimeters dilated, her doula said that she should get into the bathtub. Apparently, you had to be ten centimeters before it was safe to really start pushing and give birth, but hopefully the warm water would help relax her.

"Enough with the telling me to calm down and breathe, Brian!" Mom and I heard Sarah yelling angrily over the sound of a CD of Native American drumming. "I'd like to see *you* lie here and try and do this, Mr. I'm-Such-a-Baby-I-Think-I-Need-to-Go-to-the-Hospital-When-I-Get-a-Paper-Cut!"

Mom and I looked up from our Monopoly game. (If anything, this whole thing was letting us bank a lot of QT.) I had never heard Sarah so angry in her life. In fact, I didn't know yoga teachers were even *allowed* to get angry. She sounded even scarier than a New York City cabdriver when a car was stalled during rush hour.

"I think I said the same exact thing to your dad when I was in labor with you," Mom said.

Dad came walking out, looking like he had been through the spin cycle of a washing machine. "Boy, am I glad to see two friendly faces," he said as he joined us at that table. "Rebecca, I can't remember—did you yell at me this much when Lucy was being born?"

She nodded. "Yup."

He sighed. "I guess I blocked it out."

Mom reached over and squeezed his arm. "I'm so happy the timing worked out this way." Her eyes got so misty. "And I'm just so happy that our mutual respect for each other and our ability to communicate in an honest and authentic manner has made it so that I could share in this monumental occasion, too."

Dad got all teary, too. "I was just thinking the same thing," he said. "You have no idea how much it means to me to have you here today. Your calm manner, your positive energy—" Just as I was about to say, "Um, I hate to interrupt, but do you have any idea how long this is going to take?" Dad turned to me and grabbed my arm, too. "And Lucy, my little monkey, the fact that you get to be here for this joyous occasion—for the moment that your brother enters this world and takes his first breath—" The tears sprouted from his eyes. "There are no words to express my gratitude."

I sighed. "Since it looks like this might take a while, can we at least order a pizza from Frankie's?" I asked.

When, by three o'clock, Sarah was still only six centimeters dilated, Mom told me I had better call Beatrice and tell her that I wouldn't be at school tomorrow.

"But what happens if you win?" Beatrice asked when I told her the bad news. "The fact that the new president isn't around to give an acceptance speech doesn't really start things off on the right foot."

I put my finger over my ear to try to drown out Sarah's screaming. If she was supposedly still far away from actually giving birth, I didn't even want to *think* about what would happen when the actual pushing happened.

"I don't know," I replied glumly. "I guess I'll have to give it whenever I get back." Whenever *that* would be.

"Okay. Hey, did you post anything on the website yet about the baby being born?" she asked.

"No. Why?"

"You have to!" she cried. "It'll totally help sway the voters who are still on the fence," she said. "People love babies."

I was too tired to tell her that, actually, based on what I'd learned this weekend, that was a lie. That, really, babies were as discriminated against as dorks were.

"Too bad it's not a baby animal being born," she went on. You wouldn't happen to know anyone up there who has that going on, would you?" she asked.

"Beatrice, it's not like Northampton is made up of *farms*," I said, kind of offended. Because she had lived in Manhattan her whole life, Beatrice tended to think that anyplace outside of New York, other than Paris, was made up of cows and barns.

"Wait a second—I just had an idea. There are computers up there, right?"

I rolled my eyes. "Yeah. There are computers. We even have electricity to power them."

"If you win, you can Skype your acceptance speech!" she exclaimed. "Actually, what we can do is, I'll bring my laptop to school and I'll walk around with it so you can do some last-minute campaigning. It'll be like you're here even though you're not here."

"I don't know," I said doubtfully. For some reason,

webcams had this way of making me look like a creature from a science-fiction movie. I'd already had enough of being compared to an alien during this campaign.

"I know Friday went well, but we shouldn't think we totally have this in the bag," she warned.

"Okay, okay," I said. "But maybe we won't have to worry about that," I said hopefully. "Maybe Sarah will have the baby in the next few minutes and I can spend a half hour or so bonding with him and I'll be back by morning."

Or, then again, because I was me and things rarely ever went the way I hoped or planned, maybe I wouldn't be back. Maybe, instead, I would have been up all night because even though I finally took Mom's suggestion and took the inflatable air mattress down to the basement to try to get a little sleep, I could hear Sarah yelling all the way down there.

"What's his problem?" I asked the next morning as I tried to keep my head from falling in my cereal bowl because I was so tired. "Can't he just come out already?"

Even though she was on her third cup of coffee, Mom looked like she was about to conk out any second. She shrugged. "Water births are supposed to make it less traumatic for the baby."

But what about making it less traumatic for the rest of us? The ones who had to stay up all night and miss their school election?

Dad came into the kitchen. Now he looked like someone had taken him out of the washing machine and then run him over with a tractor. "Is she any further along?" Mom asked.

"She's at nine centimeters," he said glumly. "And she said that she doesn't want to see my face again until she's at ten."

Mom got up. "Let me see if I can calm her down a little," she said as she walked toward the bedroom.

Dad was so tired that when he sat down, he downed almost half of Mom's coffee before remembering that he had given up caffeine ten years ago. "Whoops," he said, putting the mug down. "So how are you doing, Monkey?"

"Are you still going to call me that after the baby gets here?" I blurted out.

"Sorry about that," he said. "I've been trying to break myself of that habit, but it's hard." After I turned twelve, I had told him that he couldn't call me that anymore. Especially in public.

"That's not what I meant," I said. "I meant . . . are you going to call *him* that, too?" I asked softly. "Because even though I don't really like it, it's still, you know, *my* nickname. And you can't just give a person's nickname to another person even if that other person is a cute baby."

He reached for my hand. "Honey, are you crying?"

"*No,*" I scoffed. I reached up and felt my cheeks. Huh.

Apparently I was. "Okay, *yes*," I sniffled. "It's probably because I didn't get any sleep. Sarah's loud."

"Come here," he said, opening up his arms. As I walked over, he pulled me onto his lap. Also something I had told him he wasn't allowed to do anymore. But right then, it wasn't the worst thing in the world. Especially because no one was around to see it. In fact, it felt really nice. "Of course I'm not going to call him Monkey. There's only one monkey in the world, and that's you." He lifted up my chin. "You know that, right?"

"Well, you sure haven't been acting that way," I sniffled.

He nodded. "I've been thinking a lot about what you said on the phone. And you're right. I haven't been sensitive to your needs." He turned my face toward him. "I'm really sorry, Lucy. I guess I've been a little preoccupied lately, huh?"

"Try a lot," I corrected him.

"Honey, not only are you the only monkey in my life, but you're my firstborn. My girl. And you want to know part of the reason why I meditate every day?"

"Why?"

"So I can keep my heart as big and open as possible so that there's more than enough room for you, and Sarah, and Ziggy in it," he explained. "And you know, none of the love I have for you gets taken away and given to him. In fact, it's the opposite. The more you let yourself love someone, the more there seems to be available to you."

I tried to figure out exactly how that worked in my head but because (a) it was mathlike, and (b) I was so tired, all it did was give me a headache.

"Are you willing to trust me on that one?" he asked.

I shrugged. "I guess."

He hugged me. "Good."

The next scream that came from Sarah was different than the others. It was really loud and really long, like this mating call I had once heard in an Animal Planet special about hyenas. We looked at each other. "I think it's finally showtime," Dad said, as he struggled to his feet.

"Dad?" I asked as I began to follow him.

He turned to me. "What, Monkey?"

I smiled. "Nothing. Just checking."

chapter 12

Dear Dr. Maude,

Because you've never had a baby, I'm not sure if you know this or not, but giving birth takes a lot of time. When it's finally time for me to have a baby, I'm definitely adopting. And not just because there are millions of kids around the world who need homes. I mean, who wants to spend all their time screaming and pushing something the size of a watermelon out of them when they could be doing something a lot more interesting like watching TV?

Because I've been up all night, I'm too tired to really get into it right now, but all you really need to know is that even though Ziggy wasn't supposed to get here for another three weeks, Sarah is in the process of giving birth to him right now. I haven't gone into the bathroom to see any of it because it just sounds beyond disgusting and I don't feel like throwing up at this moment. But I can tell you this: From the amount of yelling Sarah is doing, she is NOT having fun.

All I can say is I hope that Ziggy gets her really nice Mother's Day gifts throughout her life, because as annoying as she can be, she totally deserves it. I'll even help him pick them out.

Wish me luck—both with the election AND that I'm not forced to cut the umbilical cord. Because that totally would make me throw up.

yours truly,
LUCY B. Parker

I didn't throw up quite then, but I almost lost my breakfast when Beatrice walked around school with her laptop trying to get me to talk to voters.

"Um, Beatrice?" I yelled into the computer as I stared at the shaky screen. "Can you slow down a bit? I'm starting to feel like I'm on a roller coaster!"

Her face filled the screen. "Sorry. Just trying to hit as many undecided voters as possible," she replied. "Oh wait—here's Nicole LeMaire. Talk to her. She *loves* babies!"

Nicole's face filled the screen. Or at least her nose did. Should I tell her that she had something hanging out of it or not? If it were me, I'd want to know, but some people got offended by that stuff.

"Hi Nicole! How are you?!" I yelled in my most pleasant please-vote-for-me voice. "I'm not sure who you've decided to vote for, but I just wanted to say that if I were there right now—but I'm not because I'm in Massachusetts where my *totally cute baby brother is about to be born*—" I stood up and brought my laptop toward the bedroom. "Can you hear that? That's Sarah, my dad's girlfriend, screaming in pain. Anyway, as I was saying, if I were there, I'd tell you that I sure hope it's for me. Because if I'm elected president, I plan on—"

"I already cast my vote for Cristina," she said.

"Oh. Well. Okay. Good thing we live in a democracy and you're allowed to do that," I replied.

Her face left the screen and was replaced by Beatrice's ear. "Okay, this is getting boring. I know—let's go to the voting booth now and cast your vote. That'll get us a lot of press."

"It will?"

"I don't know. At least it sounds good. Alice and Malia, come on."

As the four of us moved through the hall, I started feeling more seasick, like when we had taken the ferry over to Martha's Vineyard and it had gotten all stormy and the water got all choppy and I ran over to the side and upchucked the chili dog I had just eaten.

"Okay, everyone—hear ye, here ye—Lucy B. Parker is about to cast her vote!" I heard Alice yell.

I put my head in my hands. I wasn't even there, and I still wanted to crawl under a rock. "Alice, ex-nay on the 'here ye, here ye' stuff," I called out over Sarah's screaming.

Just then Mom came running out of the room. "Lucy, it's time! He's here!"

"What?! Now? But . . . I'm not ready to be a sister!"
I yelled, all freaked out.

"Well, you can take that up with him in a few years,
after he learns how to talk," she replied. "Do you want to
see this or not?"

"Okay, we're just about to enter the voting booth,"
I heard Beatrice say. "Say something to the voters!"

It was bad enough when I had to choose what kind of
ice cream I wanted, and now I was being asked to make
this kind of decision? Talk about putting someone under
pressure. At least I knew what I was going to do.

I stood up. "Beatrice, you're going to have to cast my
vote without me. I have somewhere else I have to be."

If I found out that someone had the chance to see me
be born and her response had been "Nah, I think I'll skip
it. I'm kind of busy at the moment," my feelings would
be really hurt. Not to mention the karma that went along
with that would NOT be good.

When I got to the bathroom door, Sarah was midscream
while Dad stood beside the bathtub all hunched over
as if he was about to catch a football and Mom stood
up near Sarah's head, mopping her forehead with
a towel. And then, just as I said, "So has he finally
gotten his act together and decided to come out?"
there was this noise that sounded partly like a cry
and partly like the sound that our old refrigerator

used to make before it gave up and conked out for good.

And there he was.

My brother.

Ziggy Elias Fisher-Parker.

Or maybe not, I thought hopefully. "So now that you've seen him, are you still thinking that's the way to go name-wise?" I asked.

"*Yes*," said Sarah and Dad in unison.

"Okay, okay. Just checking," I replied.

After everyone had finally stopped crying and the doula had washed him off, and Astrid stood over him waving a feather and mumbling something that she *said* was a Native American prayer but, if you asked me, sounded a lot more like made-up nonsense, Dad called me over.

"Lucy, come see your brother."

My brother. I had a *brother*. And I would have a brother for as long as we were both alive which, because I was only twelve and he was only minutes old, would probably be a long time.

I don't know why I was so nervous as I walked over. I mean, he was just a *baby*. It's not like he could hurt me. But still, my teeth started chattering, which is something they do when I'm really nervous. My hands got all clammy, too. I really, really hoped no one asked me if I wanted to hold him just yet because while I didn't want to be rude and say no, I'm pretty sure holding a baby when your hands are clammy AND shaking was in the "Don't" column of "What to Do with a Newborn Baby."

"Do you want to hold him, Monkey?" Dad asked.

"Um, if it's okay, I think I'll wait," I replied.

"Of course it's okay, sweetheart," Mom said, squeezing my shoulder.

But I did get in a little closer so I could get a better look. And I was totally unprepared for what I found. No one tells you that newborn babies and little old men look *a lot* alike. It was probably because he had spent so much time in the womb and then in the bathtub, but this particular baby also happened to look like a raisin. However, the fact that raisins are purple, and purple just happens to be my favorite color, made me think that maybe there was hope for me and Ziggy after all.

Another thing no one tells you is that watching a baby is about as interesting as watching a goldfish. Meaning so completely NOT interesting that you wonder why you just spent your allowance on one. All they do is cry and sleep and eat and poop. And the eating part, because it was from Sarah's boob, was something I did NOT need to see.

So instead of watching that, I sat in the living room and tried not to think about the fact that any minute, I'd be getting a call from Beatrice with the results of the election. Except it turns out that trying not to think is almost as boring as thinking.

Which is why I finally turned on the TV and flipped around until I got to one of Connor's better movies—*Monkeyin' Around.* I was so caught up in watching him try to pass the chimp off as his little sister (when we were hanging out in L.A., he had told me that this particular chimp was a total nightmare and that every time it was time for Connor's close-up, he'd pitch a total fit) that I barely heard the phone ring. But when I looked down and saw Beatrice's picture on my phone screen, I forgot all about monkeys and babies and raisins.

As I clicked the phone on, I closed my eyes.

"They finished counting the votes," said Beatrice.

I knew what was coming. "Well, we definitely tried our hardest," I said glumly.

"Yup. We sure did," Beatrice sighed.

"You guys were just awesome," I said. "Seriously, not only could I have never asked for a greater campaign team, but I couldn't ask for better friends, either," I babbled. "With how hard we all worked, we really should have won—"

"Yeah. Which is why it's a good thing. . . . WE DID!" she screeched.

All the blood from my head rushed down to my feet in under two seconds. "Wait a minute—what?!"

"You, Lucy B. Parker, are the new seventh-grade class president!" she screamed.

"I . . . what . . . how . . ." I stuttered as I turned around in circles.

"She said," came another voice, "you're the new seventh-grade class president!"

I stopped turning. "Laurel? What are you doing there?"

"You think I'd miss this?" she laughed.

"But . . . you're supposed to be shooting today."

"That's one of the good things about being the star of your own show. When you ask if you can leave early because you have a family event, they kind of have to say yes," she said.

If anyone had told me a year before that Laurel Moses would leave the set of her TV show to go hang out at a school and wait for election results for me, I would've said they were completely crazy. And even crazier was the fact that when she said that she and I were family, she was right.

"So how does it feel?" she asked.

I thought about it. "It actually . . . doesn't yet," I admitted.

She laughed. "Well, let's hope it does in a half hour, because that's when you have to give your acceptance speech."

A baby brother, an election win, and an acceptance speech all in one day? How much could a girl take?

And when that baby brother is howling in the background as you're staring at a computer screen trying to Skype your acceptance speech, you feel like you can take even less.

"As I was saying," I shouted into the computer, "I am beyond grateful that the people have spoken and they have spoken me. Wait, that's not right. I mean, they have *chosen* me! And the first thing I'm going to do once I get back to school is—"

The crying got louder as Dad paced around the living room jiggling Ziggy. I turned to him. "Um, Dad? I'm kind of in the middle of my acceptance speech here," I whispered.

"What, Monkey? I can't hear you! The baby's crying!" he yelled over the wailing.

I slumped down. Great. Now the entire seventh grade knew that my dad called me "Monkey." Just what you wanted a president to be called.

"Well, can you just—" I started to say.

"I can't hear you! I'll just come over to you . . ."

Then, as he walked over, the weirdest thing happened—Ziggy started to get quiet. And by the time he was standing in front of me, Ziggy had shut up almost completely except for a few yowls here and there.

"Lucy, it's like you're a . . . baby whisperer!" he exclaimed.

Huh. It seemed like he might be right. Which would have been really interesting . . . if I wasn't *in the middle of my acceptance speech.*

But Dad was oblivious and just held Ziggy out toward me. And I just reached out and took him. It was like I couldn't control my arms, they just . . . opened. And when Dad placed Ziggy in them, it was like how those two halves of those "BFF" heart charms work. He just . . . *fit* in them. And they wrapped around him in such a way that he was really snug and there was no way I was going to drop him or touch that spot on the top of his head where I could hurt his brain.

Apparently, I knew how to hold a baby.

Who knew?

And then, the yowling stopped and turned into that refrigerator sound, and soon enough even that stopped, and then there was nothing but the *teensiest,* softest sound of air going in and out of his nostrils as he fell asleep.

I was so amazed by my magic powers that I totally forget about my speech. That is until Alice yelled "Lucy? Lucy?! Where are you? Are you okay? Did something happen? Why did that baby finally stop crying?! Is he okay?! Is he choking on something because, you know, that happens a lot to babies—they choke and then you have to do that Hemlock thingy—"

But even through all of Alice's high-pitched screeching, Ziggy kept sleeping. "Alice, he's fine," I whispered. "He's just sleeping." As I put my finger toward his tiny little fist, he grabbed it. Without even opening his eyes. The feeling of his tiny fingers wrapping around it was the coolest feeling in the entire world.

And not only that, but his skin didn't feel raisin-y at

all. Instead, it was super-soft, like my leg had been when I shaved it the first time over the summer. I looked up at the screen where I saw Laurel wiping her eyes. "If it's okay with everyone, I'd like to wait until I get back to New York to give my speech," I whispered. "'Cause right now I'd like to hang out with my brother." I looked at him. "Ziggy."

"Your brother's name is Ziggy?!" Scott Fordham yelled out.

"Yeah. What about it?" I demanded.

"That's such a cool name!" he replied.

I smiled as Ziggy clutched at my finger harder. "I know," I said proudly.

chapter 13

Dear Dr. Maude,

I don't have a lot of time to write because I have to get to school early for a meeting with my vice president Jose Cuello, followed by a meeting with the eighth-grade president Lindsay Sayles to figure out how our the two grades can get along better, followed by actual school, followed by bra shopping with Mom (ew), followed by homework, followed by a Skype session with Ziggy (basically, I talk and he sleeps in his swing—which, next to my arms, is pretty much the only place he'll do that), followed by . . . I can't even remember. Oh right—Blair is going to come over and show me how to use iMovie so I can make my own weekly presidential updates. Even though he says he doesn't mind doing them for me. Which, according to Laurel, is something that someone who has a crush back on you would say.

As you can see, my life has gotten pretty busy since winning the election, so I hope you won't feel hurt if I don't write as much. The good news is that even though my life is getting bigger, everything inside me seems to stretch to be able to fit it all. Don't worry if you can't figure out how exactly that works—I tried once, and because it's sort of like a math problem, I gave up. But I promise you, it does work.

Anyway, maybe I'll see you around the building some time.

yours truly,
LUCY B. ParKer

When I'm not busy overlistening to my mom's conversations or keeping the Official Crush Log of the Center for Creative Learning, I'm updating my Web site!

LUCYBParker.com

Check out my site for:

- A sneak peek at upcoming books
- My personal "Why Me?" diary
- The purr-fectly funny "As Seen by Miss Piggy" feature
- Author Robin Palmer's advice column (She's a LOT better at responding than Dr. Maude!)
- Fun downloadables and more exclusive content!